# NO ROCKING CHAIRS YET

The Walk and Talkers

# NO ROCKING CHAIRS YET

The Default Setting for Life After Fifty Just Got Kicked Down the Beach!

RINA TORRI

Order this book online at www.trafford.com
or email orders@trafford.com

Most Trafford titles are also available at major online book retailers.

© Copyright 2012 Rina Torri.
All rights reserved. No part of this publication may be reproduced, stored in a retrieval system, or transmitted, in any form or by any means, electronic, mechanical, photocopying, recording, or otherwise, without the written prior permission of the author.

Photographer of the front cover image: Jeffrey Van Voorhis www.VanVoorhisDesign.com

Printed in the United States of America.

ISBN: 978-1-4669-5829-6 (sc)
ISBN: 978-1-4669-5828-9 (hc)
ISBN: 978-1-4669-5827-2 (e)

Library of Congress Control Number: 2012918820

*Trafford rev. 10/11/2012*

 www.trafford.com

North America & international
toll-free: 1 888 232 4444 (USA & Canada)
phone: 250 383 6864 ♦ fax: 812 355 4082

*To all the vital women over fifty everywhere*

*May they keep on walking with courage, perseverance, joy, and laughter*

# CONTENTS

## SPRING

PROLOGUE ................................................................... xiii
1. AGING WITH ATTITUDE ........................................ 1
2. HUSBAND MORPHS INTO BACKSEAT DRIVER ......... 7
3. ANNOYING CHANGES ........................................... 11
4. BEACH WALKS ...................................................... 17
5. AGING PARENTS ................................................... 23
6. SINGLE AND FREE ................................................ 27
7. GRANDCHILDREN ................................................. 29
8. PARENTING ADULT CHILDREN ............................. 35
9. MOTHERS-IN-LAW ................................................ 39

## SUMMER

10. CASSIE'S LINE DANCE SURPRISE ........................ 45
11. AIRPLANE FLIGHTS TEST PATIENCE AND
    ENDURANCE ....................................................... 49
12. ENDLESS ASPIRATIONS ...................................... 53
13. TO-DO LISTS ...................................................... 59
14. HIGH-MAINTENANCE LADIES .............................. 63
15. DANCING AT CASSIE'S ....................................... 67
16. MIRROR, MIRROR ON THE WALL ........................ 69

17. WHAT'S YOUR WORST HAIRDRESSER STORY?........ 75
18. DECORATIVE SURGERY ................................................ 79
19. STEPFORD WIVES ......................................................... 83

# FALL

20. A CHANCE ENCOUNTER ............................................. 87
21. WEIGHTY CHALLENGES ............................................. 91
22. COOKING DINNER AND EACH GUEST IS ON A
    DIFFERENT DIET ......................................................... 95
23. INDIGESTION QUEENS ................................................ 99
24. WAITER, BRING BACK MY PLATE! ........................... 105
25. FIRST LOVE ................................................................. 109
26. STUFF ........................................................................... 113
27. LIVING WITH A PAPER PACKRAT ............................ 117
28. LETTER FROM TRENT ................................................ 123
29. FASHION CHALLENGES .............................................. 127
30. NICHOLAS ALMOST PROPOSES ................................. 133
31. BEACH LESSONS .......................................................... 137
32. PET PEEVES ................................................................. 139
33. THE "YOU GUYS" EXPRESSION ................................. 145
34. NOSTALGIA .................................................................. 149
35. CATCHING FIREFLIES ................................................. 155
36. CHRISTMAS WISHES ................................................... 161

# WINTER

37. HE KNOWS! .................................................................. 165
38. MOVING ....................................................................... 169
39. PEGGY'S PINK LADIES ................................................ 173
40. TAKE IT ALL IN ........................................................... 175
41. SPEAK, WRITE, THINK ............................................... 179
42. REALIZATION .............................................................. 185
43. TRENT'S DREAM ......................................................... 189
44. GREEN-EYED MONSTERS .......................................... 191
45. LEGACIES ..................................................................... 197

46. HOUSEWORK . . . UH, OH! .............................................. 201
47. A FULL PROPOSAL ....................................................... 205
48. HAPPY MARRIAGES ...................................................... 207
49. LOVE AFTER FIFTY ...................................................... 213
50. THE BEST IS YET TO COME ......................................... 215
51. UPLIFTING SONGS ....................................................... 219

AUTHOR'S NOTES ............................................................ 221

# SPRING

*All truly great thoughts are conceived by walking.*
—Friedrich Nietzsche

# PROLOGUE

As Peggy Conti Crawford slid out from under the comforter on her side of the California king-size bed, she decided to ignore the arthritic aches and stiffness that seemed to randomly occur in different parts of her body.

*I'll feel much better as soon as I get moving*, she knew, as she hurriedly got ready, minus any possible distractions from her husband, Mack, who was already out playing tennis. After hooking her cell phone onto the waistband of cropped pants, slathering on plenty of SPF, and popping on a wide-brimmed hat and sunglasses, she backed her Toyota out of the driveway of their one-level SoCal home and turned west toward the beach.

For almost half a year now, she'd been meeting her closest friends, Barb Demeter and Cassie Harrison, on the first and third Saturday of every month during low tide. *We're the walk and talkers*, she couldn't help but smile to herself. *Our conversations about the situations in our everyday lives have more substance than much of the chatter and prattle put together on TV. Topics just naturally come up; and then we bat them back and forth, encouraging, and supporting each other. Best of all, we're able to pull back and laugh at ourselves.*

Peggy, who had stopped counting birthdays at fifty-nine, was a reference librarian and also an avid blogger. She liked to think of herself as catching the ordinary moments of life and then posting them in the form of personal reflections for her readers to enjoy.

Despite her upbeat nature and keen sense of humor, waves of nostalgia hit her hard whenever she thought about her kindhearted Italian father, who had died one year ago at the age of ninety-four, and about her mother, who no longer recognized her. Although the petite blonde looked much younger than her calendar years, a gift of inheritance from her Danish mother, she grappled with the same challenges, changes, and concerns as other women in her seasonal range. Her long marriage to Mack, a retired accountant, had always been a solid one; but lately she was feeling restless.

Cassie Harrison, a fifty-six-year-old baby boomer and English teacher extraordinaire to high school seniors, was still reeling from the shock of being dumped a few years ago by an unfaithful husband, who preferred to live with a younger wife during the third chapter of his life. After the divorce, she'd settled into a cozy townhouse with a tropical-themed garden, vowed to stay single, and routinely spent a chunk of her summer vacations back in Baltimore visiting her parents and son, who was a med student there. On the way home, she would always stop in Pittsburgh to see her married daughter and two toddler granddaughters.

Native Californian Barb, recently retired from a long successful career as a nurse practitioner, was feeling the squeeze between her aging parents' needs and her adult children's view of her as an instant babysitter. How could she *at long last* accommodate her own aspirations—that had needed to stay on the back burner for so many years—as well as all these new demands? Being a mother-in-law, not exactly an admired position in our present culture, was no piece of cake either. Her husband Drew's hilarious quips, in rapid-fire response to her vocal frustrations, usually helped, sometimes irritated.

*I wonder that we'll talk about today,* Peggy pondered while pulling into a parking space. It was mid-April, and she loved the increasingly longer sunlit days. As she strode briskly toward her waiting friends, who were already animatedly chatting along the water's edge, she hadn't the slightest hint about the surprises and life-changing decisions that lay before them in the months to come.

# 1
# AGING WITH ATTITUDE

*Grant unto me the seeing eye, that I may see the beauty in common things . . . and that I may know that each age from first to last is good in itself and may be lived . . . happily.*
—Edmund Sanford

After Barb and Cassie greeted Peggy enthusiastically, and the three friends shared a couple of minutes of small talk, Barb launched directly into the topic on her mind.

"I see another great big birthday looming portentously on the horizon," she wailed.

"Any birthday you reach is a great one," Cassie offered, sagely.

"Don't even look at the horizon," Peggy advised, as they started to walk briskly in a southward direction from their starting point in front of the Tamarack parking lot on Carlsbad State Beach.

"I get into a room with women who qualify for senior rates, I look around, and I say to myself, *I don't belong here.* Some terrible mistake has been made. It's not possible that I've reached this stage in my life. I'm too young to be this old!" Barb continued.

"So where do I fit in? In which niche would I feel comfortable? *The young-old? The in-betweeners?*

"I feel as if I'm caught in a time warp, living somewhere after midlife and before rocking chairs."

"After fifty, we're all in an unclassified group. We're *the new unlabeled*," Cassie laughed. "Look, Barb, what you need is a little attitude adjustment. Every age has its own unique advantages, but you've got to do a search for them. Every moment is interesting in a way that will never come again—whatever age you happen to be is the best age."

"Easy for you to say," smirked Barb. "You're the youngest of us."

"Oh, come on, Barb," Cassie responded, "you know age is inconsequential, doesn't matter, after fifty. When we were very young, just a year or two made such a big difference. No longer. After a certain point of maturity, everyone has enough cumulative experience to be able to commiserate with one another."

Peggy breathed in the salty sea air and watched as a rolling wave suddenly surged. This early in the morning, prebreakfast, the air was still cool and crisp, and the ocean's deep navy blue depth lines sharply contrasted with cerulean tones. A seagull veered sharply over the swell of the surf to snatch a morsel floating with the breeze.

A pause in their discussion offered the opportune moment for Peggy to insert some hard facts. "About three years ago, a Scripps Health Study asked the question, '*Could genome research make one hundred twenty the new forty?*' Our number of years on this planet will eventually become irrelevant.

"Already, the number of persons living to ninety or more has almost tripled since 1980 and will increase to over 7.6 million in the next forty years.

"And keep in mind that our real age is not necessarily the same as our calendar age. It's as if there's a default setting for each age; well, I say, let's delete it.

"This time in our lives is referred to in so many ways—*the third age, pre-old age, the encore generation, post-middle age*, on and on. But guess what? Most women in Samoa totally ignore birthdays, and Hindu women in Orissa do not label life's stages."

"Maybe we can learn something from them," said Cassie.

"All I know is each year seems to vaporize faster," Barb resumed. "I have the sensation that someone has pushed the fast-forward button, and now I am hurtling through space and time toward the final stage."

Listening to Barb nudged Peggy's memory. "I read somewhere that these are *bonus years*, a stretch of productive, still somewhat energetic time tacked onto the tail end of middle age.

"Author Abigail Trafford tells us that increasing longevity has added this new stage of life before old age and that with these bonus years, the need comes to reinvent ourselves. We've got to write a new script for this extra period, with all of its endings and beginnings."

"The *panic du jour* is that my bonus time will evaporate before I can do everything I long to do," reiterated Barb. "The nanoseconds are racing by at breakneck speed.

"I must tell you, though," she continued, "that Drew's sense of humor keeps me going forward. When I complained to him that I'm moving much too fast through time, he quipped, 'Then that means you're in good shape!'"

After a long and satisfying laugh, Peggy had more to say. "One thing I never do is say my exact age out loud. I don't want to hear the number because then it will become too real. It will become the reference point against which I measure everything from now on—how I feel, how I look, what I want to achieve, what I'm capable of doing and dreaming."

"The most I'll admit to others is that I'm postmenopausal," Cassie threw in. "People can just categorize me that way."

"Say I feel sluggish one day," Peggy resumed. "If I subscribe to *old-think*, I might say to myself, 'Well, women this age are expected to feel lethargic,' instead of saying, 'I feel sluggish today, so I'm going to take a long, slow walk or relax in my Jacuzzi. Then I'll be refreshed.'

"Another thing—there are too many negative age-related stereotypes. I want people to focus on my character and personality, not my age. It will be easier for them to do that if they don't look at me and automatically see a number superimposed on my being.

"Besides, the promo for the cell phone I just bought says, *'You're a spunky axis with the many facets of your life orbiting around you 24/7.'* So I'm feeling pretty good about myself," she chuckled.

"Seriously, though, I like to look at the positive aspects of aging," Peggy added. "The frustrating *what-ifs* of our youth have been answered one way or another, we are finally released from the prison of obsessing about who's looking at our looks, and we can concentrate on being the kind of person we were created to be."

"These years, from fifty onward," remarked Cassie, "are not just *bonus years*, they are years in which we can become trailblazers for younger women who can benefit from the lessons we've learned. It's easier to make friends of all ages now that we are not perceived as competitors."

Barb's voice evolved from subdued to animated, evincing her otherwise imperceptible attitude readjustment. "When Drew and I were out for dinner the other night, I told him about an acquaintance's remark when I ran a bit late for a meeting. 'Well,' she told me, 'you're getting older.'

"'Next time she says that,' Drew advised, 'or if anyone else says you're getting older, just answer, *I'm trying to!*'"

When Peggy returned home, she found the old poem that had been nagging her from the back of her mind:

> *Ring the bells that still can ring*
> *Forget your perfect offering*
> *There is a crack in everything*
> *That's how the light gets in.*
>
> —Leonard Cohen

After quickly e-mailing these lines to her friends, she prepared raspberry-yogurt smoothies for herself and Mack, who was already busily engaged in his daily stock market analysis. Placing her drink at a safe distance from the computer, Peggy got started on her next blog. She was glad Mack was not standing right there behind her reading it.

# 2

*Peggy'sMoments.com*

## HUSBAND MORPHS INTO BACKSEAT DRIVER

### April

If my husband ever needs someone to drive him around again, he will have to hire a chauffeur.

Three hair-pulling, teeth-gritting, stomach acid-producing weeks as his driver-in-chief were enough to last a lifetime. Suddenly, I had been thrust into this role when he injured his right ankle while playing tennis, never dreaming his normally calm, pleasant disposition would morph into that of the proverbial backseat driver. Only he was not sitting in the back; he was right next to me in the front passenger seat, sitting rigidly, at high alert, eyes darting to and fro.

His transformation started with a little complaint at a stop sign. "You just made a California stop! You could have gotten a ticket for that. You're supposed to make a full stop, not a rolling stop!"

"I made a quick stop, true, but it was a complete stop," I reassured him, as I continued to drive along a totally deserted road.

One early morning, driving along the 101 in Del Mar, I noticed two bicyclists riding abreast about a block ahead. The one on the outside, in his purple and orange skin-tight outfit, which hid nothing but what God gave him, kept zigzagging slightly over the bike lane line. As I started to change lanes, Mack suddenly jerked his head around and sucked in his breath with such force he was lucky there were no flies around. "Why wait till you're right up on them," he complained. "Couldn't you have moved over to the left lane way before this?"

Tensions kept escalating. Sometime during week number two of my sentence, one of the traffic lights I'm well-acquainted with decided to turn yellow as I approached it at fifty miles per hour. I knew I could very safely make it through the intersection before the light would turn red. "You should start slowing down immediately when a light turns yellow so you can stop in time," Mack instructed, "not gun the engine and race through the intersection. You were just fortunate that light stayed yellow long enough; some of them change fast. One of these days, a camera's going to catch you racing through a red light."

By week three, every time I pressed the brake to slow down, Mack would jam his left foot into the floor mat, brace himself by pushing one hand against the dashboard, and stop breathing. "Where did you get your license," he asked in an exasperated tone, "at Sears and Roebuck?"

Even backing out of a tight parking space unnerved him. "You're too close; you're going to scrape our car!"

"Know what?" I responded, "I'm glad you inhaled so deeply. You narrowed our car!"

Now was a good time to listen to one of my language tapes instead of arguing. Before I pushed the start button, Mack spoke up. "That's going to split your attention. Driving is a full-time job."

"I could learn Spanish," I said.

"Yeah, the Spanish Hail Mary!" he quipped.

One evening, when Mack's ankle was almost healed, I was driving along, listening to his usual moans and groans when lights started to flash behind me. "Oh my goodness, that must be for me," I grimaced.

"Of course, it's for you. I knew you'd get a ticket one of these days," Mack barked.

The cop, who had emerged out of nowhere, as they notoriously do, asked the routine question, "Do you know how fast you were going?"

"Not fast enough; you caught me," I managed to smile. Not amused, the cop informed me that I had been driving fourteen miles over the speed limit.

"But, Officer, if you only knew what I've been through, driving my husband around for three weeks. He kept whining that I'd never get him to where he's going in one piece. I guess I pushed the pedal a bit more than usual as a reflex action."

Later that day, when we finally got back home alive, I vowed never to play his chauffeur again, and he wondered why his left foot kept hurting so much and he felt dizzy.

# 3

# ANNOYING CHANGES

*It isn't the mountain ahead that wears you out—
it's the grain of sand in your shoe.*
—Robert Service

*Once you reach this season of life, everything starts kicking in—tons of annoying, quirky, sometimes painful things both inside and out, from head to toe,* Peggy thought, as she flat-ironed the last strand of her blonde shoulder-length hair. And the list of mysterious physical changes is open-ended. It seems that almost every day, it's something else.

Time had swallowed and digested two weeks since she had seen Barb and Cassie, and she could hardly wait to expel these latest frustrations and elicit their understanding. The tide, though, was not charted to recede until midmorning, so she distracted herself by concentrating on her next blog, which covered an altogether different topic. She would post it today, right after their get-together.

"Well, ladies," Peggy began her diatribe later at the beach, "I now know that my vital organs are plugging along just fine. After being poked, prodded, and tested, I have been told by my internist that nothing horrendous is going on. Believe me, I'm thankful for that. But my complaint is that he dismissed most of my little bodily annoyances as simply part of normal aging. He had no explanation for them.

"And what do you think Mack said about my strange symptoms?"

"What?" asked Cassie.

"He just looked into my eyes, smiled, and said, 'It's the new you!'" Peggy and Cassie's full-throated laughter startled a sandpiper and it scurried away.

"At our stage," said Barb, "doctors are truly puzzled by the nebulous symptoms and vague complaints we report. They really don't know what to do with us. Subtle changes don't lend themselves to quick categorization.

"Face it, in ten minutes, doctors can't possibly know you. And it's rare to even be able to speak with physicians in between visits, guarded as they are by a battalion of nurses and receptionists armed with scripted answers that they communicate in saccharin tones of voice.

"They can only prescribe for the medical conditions that jump out at them. The rest, they either will guess at (in which case, my guess, as a nurse practitioner, is probably better than theirs) or will schedule a procedure for.

"We have to be our own health advocates and go to them prepared with precise descriptions. My internist would not even recognize me without my notebook and pen," Barb concluded.

"I'm my own doctor too," Peggy said with a wide smile. "Belgian dark chocolate pecan turtles are my new '*take two and call me in the morning*' favorites.

"The dermatologist I see got around my questions neatly when I complained about new keratoses popping up like mushrooms. He kindly looked at me and said, simply, 'It's time, Peggy, it's time.'"

Any health-related topics were right up Barb's alley and she barreled on. "Many of our aches and pains were just destined to happen. We're genetically predisposed to get certain ailments, which can be triggered at any time, sometimes suddenly."

"So you're saying that if I had never taken up running in my forties, I might not have developed chondromalacia in my knees in my fifties? That the act of running was the trigger?" asked Peggy.

"For you it appears to have been," said Barb. "What I'm trying to explain is that with certain right triggers, our predispositions descend upon us full blast."

At this juncture, Cassie jumped in. "I do know that fibromyalgia can be triggered by either physical trauma or severe illness. In my case, a car accident fifteen years ago caused the condition. After five frustrating years in and out of physical therapy, I finally was able to manage my pain. That same accident also exacerbated the arthritis in my neck (which showed up in an x-ray) to the point that it became painful for the first time in my life."

"If you already had arthritis in your neck before the trauma," confirmed Barb, "it is highly probable that eventually it would have become painful anyway, but the accident hastened the process."

"I would have been glad to wait," Cassie said dryly.

"Stone Age men and women did not have arthritis in their fifties and sixties the way so many of us do today. We must be doing something wrong," Peggy remarked.

"I look at it the same way you do, Barb," she continued. "We are programmed to develop certain maladies and malfunctions, which are quietly lying in wait, *like a crouching tiger behind a boulder* ready to pounce on us. The challenge is not to do anything that can trigger them."

"I'll keep that in mind," Cassie said.

Peggy had more to contribute. "You do realize that some researchers now say we have the ability to turn on the healing genes and even to turn off some of the bad genes. My analogy for this would be turning off the water supply to your toilet to stop it from flooding, which, unfortunately, I've had some experience in doing. The water is still there in the pipes, but it can't give you any grief."

During a pause in their conversation, Peggy watched as the ocean surf played its eternal game, breaking on the sand, rolling forward and dissolving in its own foam, then rapidly retreating under the crest of an oncoming wave.

"Here's something I don't understand, she said. "Why on earth would a postmenopausal woman still be going through temperature fluctuation extremes? Much of the time, I'm either too hot or too cold. I can't seem to maintain a steady, comfortable body temperature. Since weaning off my hormone replacement pills, I have been experiencing some of the old familiar menopausal symptoms again."

Peggy elaborated. "During the course of one night, I can go from shivering—I have to heat my nightgown in the dryer for sixty seconds before I slip it on—to feeling on fire—I must step outside on the patio in the middle of the night to cool down. And I still get occasional mood swings. At unexpected moments, I feel as if my nerves are ripped raw and exposed from head to foot. I thank God this doesn't happen often."

"What does your gyn think?" Cassie wondered.

"She tells me I'm one of a small percentage of women for whom the end of menopause does not necessarily mean the end of menopausal symptoms. Lucky me! I wonder if my symptoms will continue indefinitely."

"It took me several extra years to fully adjust to living without estrogen, too," said Barb. "For me, mood swings were the most bothersome symptom."

*Life is full of trade-offs,* Peggy thought, looking up at cauliflower clouds. *No more menopause—great, no more estrogen production—maybe not so great.*

"That's not all that kicks in at this time of life," Cassie piped in. "How about memory lapses? Sometimes while I'm driving, I suddenly ask myself, 'Where am I going?' Post-its on the passenger seat take care of that. The other day at home, I kept repeating out loud my list of things to do. By the time I got up the steps and walked back to my bedroom, I caught myself saying, 'Rinse the bedroom, air your mouth.'"

"I know exactly what you mean by the annoying changes that take place in us as birthdays accumulate," Barb commiserated.

"The first thing I find myself doing wherever I go is locating the nearest ladies' room."

As her friends joked about the desirability of sitting in an aisle seat in a movie theater, Peggy ruminated about the constant changes that occur in the cells of the human body that are not even noticed. *We are adapting all the time and don't even know it. In the same way, we have the ability to adapt to the obvious changes, the ones that jump out at us and say,* Here we are! *Life keeps changing and we keep adjusting.*

Minutes sans conversation passed with just the plaintive cries of some seagulls overhead. This time of year was referred to by locals as *gray May*, but Peggy enjoyed the overcast days every bit as much as the sunny ones.

Resuming the discussion, Peggy decided to add, "How about the procedures we need to get because of the changes going on? One we all have to go through at least once per decade is a colonoscopy. The prep is worse than the procedure. When I had mine, as part of my recent thorough checkup, I literally stayed in the powder room with a stack of magazines for three hours, cautiously advancing to the kitchen every ten to fifteen minutes for yet another glassful from the gallon jug of nauseating laxative solution. Then I would dash back to the powder room."

"Enough about us. How about the annoying changes in our husbands?" Barb brought up. "Drew has now started snoring, which doesn't bother him at all, but nettles me. When I suggested he might have a deviated septum which needs fixing, he retorted that he doesn't want anything added, subtracted, repositioned, or fixed unless absolutely necessary.

"The other night, I snuggled next to him and heard a rattling sound in his chest. 'Are you doing okay?' I asked him. 'That's my motor running,' he responded."

By now, Peggy and Cassie were almost doubled over from laughing, and Peggy secretly wished Drew could be cloned many times over. That man was a treasure.

Barb added with a chuckle, "Maybe a loss of hearing that occurs only during the night will be triggered in me, and then I won't be bothered by his snoring or rattling."

# 4

_Peggy'sMoments.com_

## BEACH WALKS

### Early May

*The art of walking is at once suggestive of the dignity of man. Progressive motion alone implies power.*
—Henry Tuckerman

### MYSTERIOUS FLOWERS

One morning at sunrise, I walked the beach, barefoot, alone. An arc of flame surged from the ocean on the distant horizon. Shafts of gold light-sped across the water. Triumphantly, the sun arose and spread its life-giving light. As I concentrated on the surrounding natural beauty, I felt as if I were on a minivacation.

Suddenly, a few yards ahead of me, a single long-stemmed, bright pink carnation, which was lying on the sand, caught my eye. Unable to resist its beauty, I bent down to pick it up. To my surprise, within another half minute or so of resuming my walk, a creamy white rose beckoned me from its sand bed. After a few dozen steps more, I spotted an exquisite fuchsia dahlia, then another rose, this one ruby red, and so on until I had gathered enough flowers for a startlingly beautiful bouquet.

Long-stemmed fresh flowers, in perfect condition, were strewn for about a one-mile stretch along the beach in a straight path where the sand was dry. Who had discarded these flowers?

The flowers were new, fresh, and lovely. They couldn't have been on the beach more than several hours, which meant they were tossed some time during the night. For what possible reason had they been so purposefully and carefully placed one at a time? Why at the beach?

Many scenarios popped into my mind as I pondered the mystery—a bridal bouquet caught by a hopeful bridesmaid who later took a solitary walk on the beach following a lovers' quarrel?

Flowers ordered to celebrate an occasion that was cancelled at the last minute?

Flowers too lovely to throw into a trash can but which were no longer needed after having served their purpose?

Possibilities begat possibilities.

## HUNGRY WALKS

I was ravenously hungry one afternoon as I started my beach walk. As a result, all the usual activity at the beach reminded me that I shouldn't have skipped lunch.

Shorebirds searched for nourishment along the ocean edge where waves caressed the sand, while seagulls hovered over the shallows of the shoreline looking for food. Pelicans skimmed swiftly over the swell of the surf, then veered sharply, yet smoothly, in the air to snatch morsels floating with the breeze. Starved sand flies buzzed hungrily around seaweed clusters on the moist sand.

Under an overcast sky, it was easy to imagine being in a dimly lit restaurant. A long, high wave crashed, spreading dozens of white lace, intricately patterned tablecloths across the shallow water.

Long thin strips of sea grass, coiled in heaps upon the sand, looked exactly like cooked spinach linguini. Clam and oyster shells reminded me of an oyster bar. Tiny crabs that scurried over the sand would grow into the delicious Dungeness crabs I so often enjoyed.

Soon everything that caught my eye was related to food: a bright orange picnic basket ready to be opened by a laughing young couple, an empty potato chip bag that had just missed the huge trash can near the rocks, and kelp bulbs the color of delicious spicy Dijon mustard that broiled in the intense heat.

A few puffy white clouds were dollops of whipped cream on top of fresh blueberries. Suddenly, the sun found a spot to break through, and the self-luminous star became an egg yolk, reminding me of the fluffy yellow scrambled eggs my husband and I love for breakfast, along with toasted bagels swished with light butter.

I hurried to the car and zipped home to my waiting refrigerator.

## MOMENTS IN TIME

One time, I just happened to be walking by the ocean when a young surfer stumbled from out of the ocean toward me screaming for help. Bright red blood was streaming down one of his legs. His leg had been cut deeply by his surfboard fin.

Some people pointed, some stared, and some kept doing whatever they were doing. The boy cursed and screamed at the top of his lungs. I ran as fast as I ever have in my life to the lifeguard station several hundred yards ahead. As I explained what had happened and quickly pointed toward the severely injured teenager, two lifeguards jumped up and rushed to help him, while another called for an ambulance.

But I wondered what would have happened to that surfer if I had not been there at that exact moment in time.

One week later, I returned to the same lifeguard station to inquire about the boy's welfare. I was told he would have died if help had been delayed even a few minutes more. His parents had left a note that said, in part, "It's not simply being in the right place at the right time, it's about also taking the right action. We thank God you did."

I thank God I was able.

# 5

# AGING PARENTS

"I feel as if I'm in the middle of a panini sandwich—pressed on one side by my aging parents who are steadily going downhill and pressured on the other side by my adult children," said Barb, as *the walk and talkers* sauntered along the beach on a hotter than usual Saturday afternoon in May. Flocks of seagulls chased the surf, feeding on small crustaceans.

"I know just what you mean," Peggy assured her. "Before Dad died and Mom had to move into assisted living, the saddest thing for me was watching my parents, who used to run circles around me and everyone else, wind all the way down. Maybe this would have been easier on me emotionally if they never had been such dynamos, running organizations, winning awards, always ready to lend a helping hand."

"My parents married young," resumed Barb. "They're only eighteen and twenty years older than I, so the clock seems to be ticking louder than ever for me as well. For the past few years, their friends and acquaintances have been dropping like asphyxiated flies in a sealed-up room, which contributes to their needing more and more of my attention to fill the vacuum.

"I help with food shopping and some errands, and now they also want Drew and me to join them for movies, art exhibitions, and other outings. I love them dearly and want to do all these things, but my adult children, on the other side of the sandwich, also need help with babysitting and a variety of things.

"On the lighter side, Drew tells me that his own parents attend so many funerals that these ceremonies have now become their new social life. In fact, so many of their friends are laid to rest in one particular mausoleum that they feel as if they are visiting everyone all at once when they go there. At the end of each month, a report is issued to all of the residents in the retirement complex: an average of twenty-nine bodies out and twenty new arrivals. Drew's quip, 'Well, don't get involved with that traffic!'"

Peggy and Cassie's soft chuckles were engulfed by the cacophony of sounds along the crowded shore, expected by mid-May.

"Well, what I'm really worried about," Cassie interjected, "is my father's state of mind. Besides being forgetful, as we all are at times, he often gets terribly confused. During my last visit to my parents' apartment in their retirement community, he and I decided to take a walk to the town center to pick up a package. Before trekking back, we sat down to rest and chat in the town center's lobby. Suddenly, Dad turned to me and asked, 'Why don't we go over to the town center now? We've sat here long enough.'

"Mom covers for him—reminds him when to take meds, repeats the same answers to the same questions, tapes TV shows for him, and operates the DVD. If anything happens to Mom, I really don't think he will be able to function.

"Over the years, Dad has been mentally rewriting the history of his side of the family, editing out all negatives and exaggerating any positives about his youth, his siblings, and his parents. According to him, everyone was wonderful; everything was perfect. Trouble is, he has repeated these family stories so often, he now believes them. If you point out some fact that disagrees with *his truth*, he gets furious."

"What is the truth about anyone of us?" Peggy asked, rhetorically. "Every time we remember something, the chemicals involved in summoning it up change it a little bit. Your father's stories might be outlandish, but we all rewrite our pasts to a certain extent because each of us sees in our own unique way. The Hottentots in southern Africa claim to see images of their tribal ancestors in the shapely tree trunks of the *Cyphostemma Bainesii* that are indigenous there."

Barb added in a comforting tone, "Don't fret too much about your father, Cass. As long as he still recognizes everyone, is able to take care of his own grooming, has a normal appetite, and does not experience a big shift in personality, he probably is okay with his current living arrangement.

"The hardest aspect of my parents' decline for me to accept," she confided, "is their emotional frailty. I can no longer pour out my burdens; instead, I must consider the weight it would place on them and the fact that they would only feel frustrated by knowing.

"For those of us who have had an extremely open and close relationship, where we were accustomed to talking everything over with our parents, no holds barred, and where they always could be counted on for solid advice and a lift, this is an especially difficult time. Now, the ones we turned to all of our lives can no longer be our sounding boards during tough times because then we would be relieving ourselves at their expense."

"Just be grateful you still have both of your parents," Peggy pointed out. "I can't tell you how much I miss my father, and my mother's condition is worsening to the point where she will soon be unable to converse with me at all."

"The number of Alzheimer's cases has skyrocketed because people are living long enough now to heighten the possibility of losing their lifetime of memories," Barb was quick to explain. "When synaptic function breaks down, death of neurons in the hippocampus follows."

"Still," said Peggy, "in a mysteriously beautiful way, my mother and I are deeply connected when we are together. There is a soul-like quality to her consciousness.

"She looks directly into my eyes, smiles, and hugs me back. Sometimes, she wants to dance. I take her arm and after a few wobbly dance steps, she needs to sit down again.

"And you know what else? My mother, even in her state, brings out a kindness and tenderness in others that they might otherwise have never known was in them."

Peggy wished she could send a message to women all over the world. It would say:

Help your parents in the winter of their lives whenever you can and rejoice that you are able. Accept and adjust to the persons they are now and treasure your unbreakable bond.

# 6

# SINGLE AND FREE

*From: Cassie*
*To: Peggy and Barb*

*Well, lady friends, if you live long enough, you see justice done. Schadenfreuen, that's what I'm feeling! As you know, David replaced me six years ago with a woman almost as young as our daughter and proceeded to increase California's population by two. Now, his wife has taken both their kids and left him.*

*This news just reached me via a mutual acquaintance, who says David's wringing his hands over the child support payments he now has to make on top of what he spends to help out our son. He wanted a different life and he got it!*

*Since way back in college, I've always lived by the credo that if a man doesn't want you, why on earth would you want him? My attitude has forever been: Let your man look and see every single other woman, no matter how gorgeous. It doesn't matter. If he's going to ever be thinking you are not enough for him, just as you are (and have worked hard to be), then the sooner he goes, the better. That's why I dumped all of David's belongings onto the driveway at the very first inkling that he was dallying with a thirty-something.*

*As for my present life, being single works just fine. I'll meet a good-looking man and I'll ask myself, why on earth, at this juncture, would I want to get saddled with making meals for and cleaning up after an aging man, maybe even nursing him through a host of health problems for the rest of our days? To grow old with someone is one thing—and it would have been wonderful—but to start out with someone when they are already of a certain age is quite another.*

*No, ladies, I'm not looking for marriage at this stage of my life. I know that some women find marital companionship fulfilling at any age, and I'm happy for them, but not this lady.*

*I'm single and free!*

# 7

# GRANDCHILDREN

Peggy was watering her collection of potted succulents the first Saturday in June when one of her neighbors, Carla, crossed the street to say hello and relate an amusing phone conversation she'd just had with her granddaughter.

"She's in France right now as an exchange student, I guess you know," Carla began. "Anyway, she was actually whining that her girlfriends and she really needed to go someplace different to celebrate her birthday in style. I couldn't believe my ears. 'But you *already are* somewhere different,' I told her."

After a hearty laugh, and complimenting Carla on the fact that she's been able to maintain an ongoing relationship with her granddaughter through every stage, Peggy made a mental note. *It's much easier to forge a bond with grandchildren while they are little, way before the hormones kick in*. Obviously, Carla had done exactly that.

*Now she's reaping the reward*, Peggy thought. Instead of merely eliciting one-word responses from her teenage granddaughter, *yes, no, hi, goodbye*, she's engaging in real conversations.

To achieve this kind of ongoing camaraderie, of course, we've got to enter our grandchildren's world with gusto, throw ourselves wholeheartedly into our new role, and enjoy it. By taking the initiative, we can become grandparents who interact, who continue to conjure up delightful projects as they grow older rather than let ourselves become disconnected grandparents who simply exist. My ten-year-old granddaughter and I still love to get together and talk and talk.

A few hours later, at Ponto Beach, where they had decided to meet for a change, Peggy repeated Carla's funny little story, as well as her own subsequent thoughts, to her friends.

"But for me," lamented Cassie, "it's going to be extra challenging to maintain a close long-distance relationship with my two toddler granddaughters. Whenever I get enough time off to fly to Pittsburgh, the three-day rule for fish and guests goes out the window. I stay at my daughter's house a long time, during which I knock myself out. By the time I return home, I'm ready for rehab."

"As much as I deeply love my grandchildren and want to stay bonded with them, just like you," interjected Barb, "I have an issue with spending big chunks of my time babysitting. Don't get me wrong. When I'm with my older son's three little ones, I rediscover old games, recall nursery rhymes, play beach ball catch, and swing them around. I completely immerse myself in their world, and I love doing so.

"But here's a typical example of what's happening now with my son's children. I was right smack at a critical point in my watercolor painting the other day when my daughter-in-law dropped by without any notice and plopped the kids in my hobby room just so she could have a child-free shopping day. She assumed this would be fine with me since my own son (her husband) expects me to be the ever-welcoming, indefatigable grandmother, entertaining, cooking for picky palates, and cleaning up after the kids.

"His attitude is obvious: *What kind of grandmother wouldn't be ecstatic about spending time with her very own flesh and blood?*

"Actually I'm the one who has made the mistake of letting my son and daughter-in-law assume I will babysit at any time, for any reason, even a frivolous one, with little or no notice. After seven years of putting up with this, I've been drained dry and I've had it!

"Of course, there are situations in which grandmothers must care full time for their grandchildren—there's no other way—that's a whole other story. It's understood that I will always drop everything for an urgent reason, but . . ." Barb's voice trailed off.

"Yes, but . . . ," said Peggy in complete understanding.

"But you'll be better and stronger when you are with them if you take care of yourself also," added Cassie.

"Centering my life around childcare is not the way I dreamed of channeling my postretirement energy. As you know, ambitions are eating at my gut, compelling me to get going and achieve them. Time is slipping away," Barb continued.

Peggy took some time to think before responding. A seagull, safely perched on a rock, eyes transfixed, was the portrait of composure and dignity. The lively banter and gestures of the three women had attracted its attention, and it looked at them inquisitively.

"Ideally," Peggy said, "we should decide (and announce) how often and under what circumstances we will babysit before any grandbabies are even born. This way, no one's surprised later on when we have to say no, and resentments can't build because of a false sense of entitlement to unlimited childcare.

"Don't feel bad though, Barb; plenty of soft-hearted grandmothers learn a little late in the game that they need to draw a line. Why don't you tell your son you cannot continue to be an on-call babysitter, except for emergencies? You need reasonable notice; then, if you're feeling up to it and available, you'll be happy to babysit."

Barb had more venting to do. "While I was at Barnes and Noble Bookstore recently," she told us, "I got into a conversation with a woman who said she lives for being a grandmother, that no amount of time spent with her grandson is too much. She's always trying to arrange time with him and feels hurt when her daughter says that he's busy. She is definitely on the opposite end of the spectrum from me."

"Look at the total picture," Peggy shot back. "That lovely grandmother is the one totally in control of time slots with her grandson; she takes the initiative. No one is telling her when she must take care of him. Also, she herself has made the decision that this is her mission, her calling, and she is fulfilled in achieving it."

Finally reaching Moonlight Beach, they turned around and headed northward, back to their starting point at Ponto Beach. Dozens of people of all ages were happily paddle boarding while farther out at sea, tourists jammed the deck of a sightseeing yacht and a couple of sailboats skimmed the water. From his home on top of the bluffs, a man descended the eighty or so steps down to the wide sandy shore.

"What do you think about this?" Cassie suddenly asked. "My son left a message last night asking me to take care of his Golden Retriever while he's in Maui for ten days with three other Johns Hopkins medical residents. He figures I can pick up the dog during their plane change in LA." *The subject had abruptly changed to dogsitting.*

"His dog is not even reliably trained, so I would have to dog-proof my home. I'd also wonder what the dog was getting into while I'm at work," she explained.

Peggy was quick to answer. "Do not under any circumstances or pressure take in the dog.

"If you do this favor once, you will be expected to do it for every trip your son takes. The first time you have to say no, you will become an ogre. All your past good deeds and sacrifices will be erased from your son's memory. You will be cheating him of something which you now owe him. How dare you!"

"Listen, Cass," added Barb, "you have carefully carved out a full and productive life since you sold your big house and moved into your townhome. You're finally free.

"Help your son in other, more important ways. The dog either has to stay with someone else, go to a kennel, or simply *has to go*! It's your welfare or the dog's. And anyway, tell your son the dog would be left alone much of the time. If that doesn't work, tell him right out that such an arrangement would impinge too heavily on your lifestyle, that you need to conserve energy so you can be available to your family for other needs.

"I just thought of something else," she threw in. "What if the dog is a barker? He could disturb neighbors with whom you've cultivated a good relationship."

"Wow, Barb, you've really cut to the core!" Cassie observed.

"That's it, I'm finished fussing," Barb breathed out. "But our children's attitude that their convenience counts more than our comfort and peace is misdirected.

"We have lives too, and we want to be able to live them."

Peggy couldn't wait to write the rough draft of a blog she had been putting together, off and on, for the past couple of weeks. After touching bases with Mack, who was out back, busy painting the columns and wood boards of their patio cover, she opened the shutters in the study and sat down in front of her computer.

# 8

*Peggy'sMoments.com*

## PARENTING ADULT CHILDREN

### Early June

Practically all the fifty-, sixty-, and seventy-year-olds I know say their adult children are far more challenging to deal with now than during their adolescent years.

Seemingly endless issues have these parents filling prescriptions for anti-anxiety pills and grinding their teeth at night. Here's a short list of comments about their adult kids.

"They moved out years ago but still stack bulging boxes in our garages and crowd our closets with their stuff. If they occasionally remove a few things, don't get your hopes up. They'll be back to replace those few items with even more stuff."

"Their attitude is *I can do whatever I want, it's my life, and don't give me your opinion.* That would be just fine with me and actually a welcome relief—just as soon as they start taking care of themselves 100 percent of the time. The trouble is that their mistakes impact *our lives* directly. We not only have the emotional burden of witnessing disruption in the lives of those we love, but we often are stuck paying some of the consequences for their poor choices. It's easy to say, *let them make their own mistakes.*"

"While we sacrifice *our own lifestyle* to help our adult children cope with their latest 'financial crisis,' they're drinking $4.50 lattes, working out at the gym, and going on a vacation that we can only dream about. ('Mom and Dad, if I don't get a break soon, I'm going to crack under the stress.') No wonder they run out of money for their basic necessities!"

"We had money put aside to have our house painted this year, but now those funds will be helping our son rebuild his business. We didn't mention what we're giving up, and he didn't ask."

"What I wonder is if my two adult kids, both married with children of their own, will ever get to a place where they would be able to help us out *if we needed it.* Fat chance!"

"Who would have ever believed our parenting would go on and on like this? I'm still trying to guide, to teach, and to keep them from falling over a cliff. If it's not one, it's the other, hanging on by a fingernail—how much drama can I take?"

"I used to write my schedule down in ink; now, I write in pencil and keep an eraser handy. My cell phone rings and it's another dilemma. Are they addicted to chaos?"

"I'll tell you one thing, the empty nest syndrome is a myth. I only hope my nest stays empty and that my grown son does not move back in. He would be impossible to live with again."

"We've adopted our own lifestyles and formed a multitude of little habits. Some parents find a way to cope with their adult children, as well as their grandchildren, all living together under one roof, but I'm sure it causes a complete upheaval for each person involved."

"I'd like to go up in a balloon and fly over the earth simply to observe. No participating in anything. Would you like to come along? It would be great for our health."

"Will it ever be my turn?"

Well, dear readers, I could go on, but you get the point: Parenting is endless. We change, they change, our relationships change. There are always new challenges, and there is glory in facing and conquering them.

Bring them on!

# 9

# MOTHERS-IN-LAW

"Is this a magical time? Really? Thinning hair and brittle nails aside, I've been turned into the dreaded mother-in-law by my children," Barb ranted.

"I mean, how can I possibly contend against the deeply ingrained view of mothers-in-law in this country? Never mind that much of the rest of the world honors their elder relatives and in-laws."

Barb, Cassie, and Peggy had just left the San Diego Museum of Art, where they had thoroughly enjoyed a special exhibition of postimpressionism. It was the third Saturday in June, and as they headed toward the rose garden, they were able to fit in their usual walk and talk here at Balboa Park instead of at the beach.

"It's true," Peggy said, "that our culture does not regard mothers-in-law very highly. Sitcoms and stand-up comedians love to build jokes around us. Even the *Mother-In-Law's Tongue* plant was so-named because of the sharpness of its blades."

"The wise among us pariahs follow the sage advice: *Speak softly and wear beige*," continued Barb. "But I'm not that wise.

"I read your blog about adult children, Peggy, and it was so true. If our children's decisions didn't affect us, some of them more dramatically than others, maybe we wouldn't get so discombobulated."

"You could try humming 'Tiptoe Through the Tulips' when issues come up with your children and their spouses, instead of clenching and gnashing your teeth," grinned Cassie.

"Here's another point of view, the one I'm taking," Barb said in a decisive tone. "No matter what we do or say, or what we don't do or say, we will be criticized by someone, sometime. So we might as well go ahead and enlighten our children and their spouses.

"I really exploded in front of Drew yesterday about this very subject. 'I'm no longer keeping quiet,' I shouted, 'and what good has it done me or anyone else when I have? I'm going to speak up from now on. Everything's coming out of me before I drop dead!'

"'Well, it usually does,' Drew replied."

The three women had a good long laugh and then paused long enough from their conversation to enjoy the fragrance and delicate beauty of the multicolored roses in the garden.

As they left and headed to the parking lot, Cassie spoke first. "Barb, I'm sure you've heard that moms-in-law can help their married children more effectively by standing back from the cauldron of boiling water and extending a steady hand than by leaping into the pot with them. And as you yourself have said before, you have to care for your own soul and spirit before you can console others."

"I vote for speaking up—diplomatically, calmly, and firmly," Peggy said.

"Of course, there are times in life when you literally can't speak up," she added, veering to another subject.

"Last Tuesday, while my dentist was drilling to remove the decades-old silver filling from a cracked molar, he kept spouting his extremist political views. His rhetoric kept my mind off the fact that my tooth was being prepped for an expensive crown, but it also infuriated me. I was ready to offer my point of view during a brief respite. Then I realized this was neither the time to speak up nor the person with whom to debate. He who wields the drill gets a free pass."

Mack was in the living room with their granddaughter when Peggy walked in, patiently coaxing a light brown spider onto a sheet of white paper. "It's moving day for you and you're going to love your new home in our garden. Promise," he said as Annie watched, eyes transfixed.

"Oh, your granddad always takes insects back outside," Peggy said, giving Annie a big hug. Four board games were stacked at one end of the kitchen table and the three of them were planning a fun night together right after dinner.

# SUMMER

*The moving landscape provides an absorbing diversion which frees the mind and gives us a fresh viewpoint, and we're most at ease with the world when we walk because everything is happening at a manageable pace.*

—Lloyd Jones

# 10

# CASSIE'S LINE DANCE SURPRISE

*Letters should be easy and natural, and convey to the persons to whom we send just what we should say if we were with them.*
——Philip Chesterfield

<u>From: Cassie</u>
<u>To: Peggy, Barb</u>

*Dearest friends,*

*You won't believe how I embarrassed myself during my very first line dancing class at the community center on Monday night.*

*I don't know what I was thinking when I signed up for it. That I was graceful and sure of foot? That line dancing is an easy way to flex mind and body at the same time?*

*Anyway, about forty-five minutes into the class, which by the way was packed, I must have lost my focus for a second as the instructor called out the dance steps. I suddenly spun around in the wrong direction and grapevined (one of the most basic steps) right smack into the man directly behind me.*

*For the flash of a moment, I felt as if I were stapled to the dance floor as I told him how sorry I was. With a wide smile, he said to keep on dancing, that I would do fine. Can you imagine a nicer reaction? I mean, I really slammed into his midsection.*

*I know what you two are thinking and yes, he's also good looking, large framed, and has thick salt and pepper hair.*

*Here's the 4-1-1 on him:*

*His name is Nicholas Korba. He is a computer programmer and a widower.*


From: Barb
To: Cassie
Cc: Peggy

*The only time I would bump into someone charming would be when I'm not wearing any makeup. Meeting a man this way? I don't know, Cassie, you were definitely out of line!*

*I told Drew that line dancing is great for improving mind-body connection and maybe for helping to prevent symptoms of Alzheimer's.*

*His response was, "As long as you don't forget the steps!"*

*Classic Drew.*

*From: Peggy*
*To: Cassie*
*Cc: Barb*

*After you get to know Nicholas a little more, you might want to invite him over to practice some of those new line dances.*

*I've got to book a flight to Carmel, Indiana to see my mother next month. Check out my next blog, which I'll be posting in a few days, to find out how I feel about airplane travel.*

*See you soon, dear friend.*

# 11

_Peggy'sMoments.com_

## AIRPLANE FLIGHTS TEST PATIENCE AND ENDURANCE

### July

Just the thought of an upcoming trip by airplane and I can easily contemplate the addition of a tenth circle around Dante's *Inferno* where the eternal punishment would consist of boarding airplanes, enduring long flights, deplaning, and then starting the whole process all over again.

Say you've got a flight scheduled to leave at 8:00 a.m. You've got to subtract four hours from that time to figure out what time to get up—4:00 a.m. This gives you an hour to get ready, an hour to drive to the airport and find parking, and up to two hours before your flight to check in, grab a three-dollar banana, and visit the restroom.

Ah, yes, the restroom! This is where a toilet can suddenly start flushing with such force that its contaminated water splashes your exposed skin before your pants are pulled back up. Of course, the sensors that activate the flushing, hidden underneath the tile flooring, can be in an unknown spot. In that case, you might make it to the door, start to unlock it, and then get splashed, this time all over the back of your outfit.

When it's finally time to board the plane, my anxiety level increases. Whom will I sit next to this time—a rumpled unshaven man who coughs and sneezes throughout the entire trip, ensuring that I will come down with whatever he's got within a day or two? A sixty-something woman wearing a purple acetate top who rambles on about her "noncommunicative" son as I, her captive audience, continue to stare at the same page of my book? An aging hippie who cleans out his mouth with his forefinger, first on one side, then the other, after eating a bag of peanuts?

Once, I was seated next to an athletic-looking young woman whose eyes were fixed upon the Pepsi I was about to drink as she informed me that the airline attendants neither rinse nor wipe the tops of soda cans before they pop them open. "Just think," she told me, "whatever dust or dirt that resides inside the circular groove of those can tops gets washed right into these little plastic glasses as they pour our drinks."

"You're right," I agreed, "and you can also *just think* about all the viruses and bacteria that are circulating in this airplane cabin. Better cover your sandwich with a napkin to protect it from all the microbes hovering around it."

Not to be topped, she proceeded. "The headrest of your seat could be covered with lice from the previous passenger's hair, and you wouldn't even know it. That's why I always cover the headrest with a throwaway cloth I bring from home."

Now I have to admit that her warning did get me to thinking. Why don't airlines provide clean soft paper covers that fit over the headrest portion of the seat? Too expensive? How about just dispensing them upon request? Only the very health conscious would ask.

The aisle seat used to be my first choice. I could get up every hour or so to stretch and walk up and down the aisle, thus decreasing the chance of clots, without having to squeeze past any fellow passengers' knees.

Now my first is the window seat for two good reasons: During one trip, a passenger in an aisle seat was clobbered on her neck and shoulder by a heavy piece of luggage, clumsily pulled down from the overhead compartment by a man in a hurry; and during my most recent flight, the attendant actually reached over me with a scalding hot cup of coffee, intended for the person next to me, after the pilot had acknowledged, loud and clear, a sudden patch of turbulence. Luck was with me that time.

Shortly after I take my window seat, I wonder whether the plane will take off on schedule or be forced to wait on the tarmac for four other planes lined up ahead of it. Then I will miss my connection again. Oh, and think of all the exhaust fumes.

When the attendants come around with snacks, I decline, having brought my own. Isn't it amazing that whatever they offer will be super high in sodium, saturated fat, sugar, and artificial ingredients I never heard of? And even more astounding is that people still eat them.

You can tell a lot about a person by the way he/she eats and by their food choices. If they gobble the greasy chips and chomp the high-calorie cookies, or if they hold their sandwich with unwashed hands and lick their fingers afterward, they just might not be health conscious.

Unobtrusively observing the eating styles of passengers can even become a form of airplane entertainment. Those who read while eating must have strong digestive systems. The ones who wolf everything down noisily are not sensitive to others around them, while the ones who pause between bites have manners.

It's easy to spot someone who chews with his mouth open, crumbs falling on his lap, or a person who takes bites so huge, he fills his mouth to capacity.

Since I must continue to fly to visit distant relatives and friends, I am trying to develop an optimistic, *bring-it-on* type of attitude. My plan is to spend the entire week before any future trip buttressing my immune system. Then, any self-respecting germ on an airplane would be a fool to even try to take on my vitamin C-overdosed cells.

# 12

# ENDLESS ASPIRATIONS

*Everything that you seek is seeking you.*
—The Fragile Thread

"For years, I put up with the question, 'When are you going to retire?'" Barb fumed.

"And now that I finally have retired, the automatic question popping out of everyone's mouth ad nauseam is, 'What do you do now?'"

"The *What do you do now*? question also plagued my retired sister until she came up with the perfect answer," Peggy quickly recalled.

"Just smile and say, '*Nothing.*' Then watch your questioner squirm and stammer for a comeback."

"Look," Barb continued, still a bit defensively, "I'm busy trying to fulfill many longtime aspirations; I'm retired from work, not from life. And I'm not about to explain or justify the use of my own time to anyone else."

"Truth is the three of us lead very full lives," Peggy added, signaling to their waiter that they were ready to order lunch. She and Cassie had taken Barb to a tony Italian restaurant on a Friday night in July to celebrate her recent retirement from a long and successful nursing career.

"Actually, there's so much I can't wait to do, things that had to wait when I was working full time," Barb resumed.

"So this is my plan: Learn to play the "Pineapple Rag" on the piano, write an open letter to pass down to my family about life lessons learned, e-mail senators and reps about issues important to our country's survival, volunteer once a week at the hospital, and learn Italian so I can treat my two teenage granddaughters to a tour of Italy next summer."

"During free time, I'll read my stacks of books and magazines, organize all of our loose photos into boxes or albums, and decide which of our hundreds of old slides are worth transferring to DVDs."

"What? No life-threatening adventures?" Peggy teased. "No mountain-climbing, bungee jumping, or parachuting from planes?"

"Haven't you noticed that things you thought you wanted, you don't want anymore, things you worried about, you don't now?" Cassie asked Barb and Peggy. "I don't even know the woman I was at twenty-something."

"According to Goethe," ventured Peggy, "each ten years of life has its own fortunes, its own hopes, its own desires."

"We exist for much, much more than simply to eat and drink, urinate and defecate, reproduce, and sleep. That's what cockroaches do, and surely we're on a higher level than they."

"I just want to retain my curiosity—about life, about everyone, and everything," said Cassie. "If my desire to learn ever disappears, I'll join the legions of the walking dead—motion without meaning.

"My ex used to say he had seen enough cities in his lifetime and that they are all homogenized anyway. Fool that I was, I listened to him, and we didn't do much traveling. Of course, now his young wife is dragging him all over the globe. That's okay, now I'm psyched to set foot on all the continents," she laughed, enjoying her own joke.

"Whether I get to do that or not is another story. What I do realize is that we can choose to plunge into the so-called ordinary chores, errands, and activities of everyday life with zest. Run your house creatively, cook creatively, garden creatively—you get the idea. Everything becomes interesting."

"Walk and talk creatively. That's what we do," smiled Peggy.

During a pause in their conversation, while Barb and Cassie were in the ladies room, Peggy sat at the table and thought of the endless things to do and learn. Each month, she selected a library book in a different subject area. This month, it was archeology, and so far she'd discovered the mysterious underground churches of Lalibela, Ethiopia, that were hewn in volcanic rock ten centuries ago.

There's nothing quite as satisfying as the pursuit of knowledge for its own sake. The pursuit, in itself, is the joy. The word "bored" does not exist in my vocabulary, never did, she realized. Yet there are those who vehemently proclaim they wouldn't know what on earth to do all day if they weren't working at a job outside of the home.

Of course, none of my projects is meant to lead to boosted status or monetary windfalls. Isn't that what everyone else wants? Even in Tehran, people pay to have parakeets strut along a line of folded papers and peck out missives that tell their futures: fame and fortune, long lives, marriage.

But I remember the nuns' frequent refrain back in high school: *Mankind's wants are never satisfied.* With each new monetary level attained, there's the next plateau beckoning, even more tantalizing than the one before.

Fame, as well, provides only a temporary high. While it's true that mankind has always wanted to say, "I was here!" (a Spanish cave painting of handprints was recently proved to go back over forty thousand years), I have discovered that the end of my desire to be applauded has set me free. Now I do for the love of the doing, not for applause and marching bands. Anyway, how important is it to be remembered by total strangers? Wouldn't a better legacy be a place in the hearts of those whom we have truly loved?

Almost immediately after Barb and Cassie returned, the waiter brought lunch, and Barb resumed the conversation as they started to eat.

"You know what? I have been having alternating nightmares: In one of them, I am trying to grasp at something nebulous, unidentifiable, and evasive. In the other dream, I am trying to get from one location to another and no matter what I do, I cannot reach the desired destination. Whether I board a train, bus, cab, or drive myself, something always goes wrong, and I cannot get there."

"Let me put on my psychologist's hat for a minute to analyze your dreams," offered Cassie, laying down her fork. "You're grasping at vestiges of your younger self because you are panicked about which will go first—your energy or your drive. And what if one or both of these go before you've fully developed into the perfect version of yourself?

"Age didn't stop Renoir," Cassie continued, "and it's not going to stop us. He pioneered Impressionism before he was forty and then later, at age seventy-two, he proclaimed, 'I'm starting to know how to paint. It has taken me over fifty years' labor to get this far, and it's not finished yet.'

"Feisty Grandma Moses started painting in her late seventies, became famous at eighty, and lived to age one hundred one."

"Barb," Peggy sympathized, "don't worry too much about your time running out. Each of us is here for a purpose and that purpose will be fulfilled.

"But watch out!" she grinned. "Once we do achieve our purpose, whatever it may be, we're up for grabs. So . . . don't be in too much of a hurry to get everything done."

After the table was cleared, luscious zabagliones and cappuccinos were set before them.

"Well, I'll tell you one thing," Peggy said, "Renoir and Grandma Moses might not have lost steam in their old age, but I'll bet neither one of them always got every single thing done that was on their to-do lists."

"Oh, I almost forgot. I've got to call Drew to pick me up because my car is in the shop," Barb exclaimed.

"I can swing by your house," offered Cassie.

"Thanks anyway, but after he drove me here, Drew stayed in the area to do some errands of his own. He can be here in no time," she said, while pressing his speed dial number on her cell phone.

By the time the women paid and reached the door of the restaurant, they could see Drew approaching from his car.

"It's been a while. Good to see you," smiled Cassie.

"Hi, Drew, we just had the best time together," said Peggy. "How's your day going?"

"Every day's a good day if you wake up, and if you don't, you don't have to worry about it."

Drew's quip got all of them laughing, a great way to end the day.

Peggy was thankful that Mack had taken care of his own dinner while she was out, and as soon as he settled back in his recliner to watch a favorite business news show he had taped earlier, Peggy headed for the study and began to type. Her next blog would be a no-brainer.

# 13

<u>Peggy'sMoments.com</u>

## TO-DO LISTS

I've come to the conclusion that I will never get everything accomplished in this lifetime that I want to do, have to do, and should do.

Case in point: I leafed through my 1998 schedule book, which I discovered at the bottom of a box while attempting to clean our garage, and at least four of the identical things I'm still struggling to get done were in that book. It gets worse. Not only have the same *unreachable stars* followed me from year to year, but new *unreachables* have sprung up to form a galaxy of undone things.

Next, I took a look at last year's schedule book to analyze where my time has gone. Bottom line: it was swallowed up by a host of multifaceted little things that are not even measurable, things that defy you to classify them. The interminable, self-perpetuating, never-ending to-do lists *rule*.

First, there is the grand master list of all my projects and, of course, the sub-lists of steps to be taken for each project. Then come the shopping and errands list that I carry with me, birthday and important dates lists, the bills to be paid list, as well as the Post-its all over the house. What I need now is a list of my lists!

The undone things follow me around and haunt me, just the way that black cloud always hung over one of the characters in the old *Lil'Abner* comic strip.

With a smile, my husband asks me, "Are you spending more time on the doing or on the listing?"

"Probably on the listing because the doing has become too frustrating," I fuss.

Everyday living is riddled with so many time-and-energy-zapping moments; it's semi-miraculous when you can accomplish any project that transcends the mundane. To make a simple phone call and reach a human being, you have to first get past menus, submenus, and Burt Bacharach. When you do reach a person in real time, they want to transfer you to another department.

It practically takes an act of Congress to get anything done right anymore. To get something, anything, repaired, you've got to wait out the "window of time" during which a repair person might arrive. When and if they do, you know deep down that it's highly unlikely they will fix it correctly the first time. No, there will usually be a second or third visit.

I can't even tell when my car will reach downtown San Diego in heavy traffic, but scientists know to a fraction of a second when Venus meets the sun every one hundred twenty-two years. I'm in the midst of doing all the funding of our revocable trust, trying to figure out which plans are best for our mobile phones and house phone, and learning to cohabit with my temperamental computer. If it were not for the joy of blogging, I'd have my way with this Gateway Table Top and hoist it out of the window.

Simplify life? Really? When passwords are different for every single account?

It took me three nights to wade through the user guide to my new cell phone so I can send pictures, download help menus, program different ringer tunes for each contact, and give voice commands that work. (Speaking of electronic devices, did you know they actually disrupt our natural biorhythms, our energy levels? Their electromagnetic fields release chaotic energy, according to an article in a scientific magazine.)

These days, you'd better bring along a carefully prepared list of questions, as well as comments based on your own investigative research, when you go to see your doctor. This list will increase your odds for a productive visit during the ten minutes you're lucky to squeeze out of your clock-watching doctor's day.

You'd also better be ready to do everyone's job for them. Your doctor might be on the ball, but if his secretary sends his order for therapy to the wrong place, who do you think will have to take time out to locate and then tell her the correct fax number? And will the secretary be apologetic? Come on.

One of my recent communications with an insurance agent went like this:

> Agent: That's not in your contract.
>
> Me: Look on page 24, under B 3.
>
> Agent: Oh, there it is!

Of course, the important and the urgent things must be done. But I read somewhere that the speculative and imaginative things you would like to do "someday" aren't worth the constant angst of carrying around, copying and recopying. A list is not a life sentence.

So I guess that just because I have wanted to do something for years doesn't mean it is still worth doing. I'm going to have to reassess my master to-do list. Here's to the *survival of the fittest*!

# 14

# HIGH-MAINTENANCE LADIES

*There are no better cosmetics than . . . a gracious temper and calmness of spirit.*

—John Wray

"Wouldn't it be wonderful if we could just get up in the morning and be completely ready to dive into our day? Imagine—no lotions or potions, treatments, or rituals!" Cassie beamed.

"All I can say is it's taking me longer and longer to get ready in the morning," Peggy said. "I'm becoming so high-maintenance that in a few years the *getting ready for the day* block of time and the *getting ready for bed* block of time will eventually meet, right smack in the middle of the day.

"While it's true that vanity is programmed into the software of our humanity, I spend too much time in front of the mirror already trying to thwart time. I don't want to add one more thing to my beauty regimen. How many years would it total if we added up all the time spent trying to be a head-turner, evaluating every wrinkle and inspecting each new age spot, applying and removing makeup?"

"Trouble is," chimed in Barb, "as time goes by, more and more maintenance is required. Where would I be without my age-defying makeup and hair-sculpting foam? Then there's my toning and stretching routine, making the effort to eat right, and keeping track of my calcium, glucosamine sulfate, D3, and fish oil tablets, as well as the flaxseed and almonds I've got to ingest during the course of a day.

"I had some photos taken recently, and they gave me a shocking reality check. 'Look at all the wrinkles,' I complained to Drew.

"You know what he said? 'One wrinkle cancels out another. You look great.' What a sweetheart!"

"Realistically, is there any way we can simplify our maintenance regimen?" Peggy dared to ask, as the three women slowed to a more contemplative pace on this first Saturday in August. Reddish brown jellyfish of all sizes had been washed ashore and were scattered along the waterline, some tangled within large clumps of kelp. The sun was a flaming disk, and they were all glad they had worn hats.

"Oh, come on," said Barb, "I've got to do everything possible to look decent, what with crow's feet and laugh lines. When I got up this morning at zero-dark-thirty, I laid my magnifying mirror down flat on the bathroom counter to get a closer look at a new brown spot on my forehead. Then I bent down over the mirror. A big mistake! Undiplomatic gravity dealt my ego a fatal blow as everything dropped forward. Loose skin I didn't even know I had!

"On top of this early morning shock, I'm so tired I dragged myself here today. Drew got up at least four times during the night, and each time he got back into bed, he struggled with his pillows till he got them into the exact position to cushion his knees and lower back. By the time he was all cozy and settled, I was wide awake," she added, as they passed by a large surf camp canopy where two instructors were setting up for business.

"Maybe we could simplify our routines by eliminating some of the so-called firming creams," offered Cassie.

"It's emotionally exhausting to consider all the choices advertised in a typical magazine today," Peggy agreed. "If I did everything being pushed, that's all I'd be doing with my life all day, every day.

"Think about it: If you were marketing a new facial cream, wouldn't you be sure to use the trendy adjective '*firming*' somewhere in its description? Maybe these creams do nothing, and our skin keeps on *firmly sagging*. As the grinning Cheshire cat proclaimed, in *Alice's Adventures in Wonderland*, 'A word is what I say it is at any given time.'

"Well, I guess the time will come, at some point in our lives, when we will decide to stop evaluating every wrinkle and inspecting each new age spot, when we will finally will break free from feeling the need to apply, remove, and reapply makeup."

Barb was not about to even consider such a time. "I remember the exact moment I was applying lipstick and suddenly realized that my slowly-disappearing lip line was completely gone. Where did it go? Did it recede into my face? Lip liners used to be optional makeup tools; now I absolutely must use them for definition."

"There's always so much stuff laid out on my bathroom counter when I'm getting ready that one morning I accidentally reached for the Colgate, instead of the Bacitracin for my nose infection, and massaged toothpaste into my left nostril," Cassie said, causing Peggy and Barb to burst out laughing.

Peggy could hear Mack and their son Alex in the kitchen having one of their animated money talks as soon as she approached the entry door from the garage. *For financial advice, Mack's the best*, she thought.

Not wanting to disturb their special time together, she called out a cheerful greeting and decided this was a perfect time to catch up on her reading pile. She could fix some sandwiches for them in about an hour and enjoy Alex's company then.

# 15

# DANCING AT CASSIE'S

<u>*From: Cassie*</u>
<u>*To: Peggy, Barb*</u>

*I finally took your suggestion to heart and invited Nicholas over for dinner and line dance practice. I prepared Irish stew, following a recipe handed down by my grandmother, only I used very lean beef, trimmed of fat and gristle, and a larger proportion of vegetables. Nicholas brought flowers for the table and fresh plump blueberries for dessert.*

*We thoroughly enjoyed talking with each other, and then, after dinner, we reviewed the trickiest line dances, the ones with intricate choreographies, until we got them down pat. We had the best time ever, punctuated with a large dose of laughter.*

*And no, the bedroom was not calling to us. He left about 11:30 and somehow I knew we were an item.*

*From: Peggy*
*To: Cassie*
*Cc: Barb*

*Sounds like the beginning of a beautiful friendship.*


*From: Barb*
*To: Cassie*
*Cc: Peggy*

*Or a beautiful romance!*

# 16

# MIRROR, MIRROR ON THE WALL

*Must we forever be the fairest of them all?*

While it's only natural to want to look our best, how can we prevent our mirrors from taking control and dominating our lives?

This topic had been on Peggy's mind since their last walk and talk, so she jumped into it as soon as she and her friends met again. Red tee-shirted lifeguards floating on their multicolored boards added to the natural attraction of the sea.

"Look, the number of image-repair choices (potions, lotions, serums, volumizers, plumpers, gels, fillers, microdermabrasers, and miracle creams), all packaged to entice, can be overwhelming, even stress-producing," she told them.

"Then there are the injectables (Botox, Restylane, collagen, Sculptra, Radiesse, silicone, and fat), as well as laser therapy for facial veins, laser resurfacing, intense pulse light facials, facial waxing, oxygen and acne facials, peels . . . the list goes on and on.

"Even at a spa, a barrage of topical tonics promises to invigorate, rehydrate, detoxify, renew, nurture, reveal, and relax skin, body, and mind.

"Where do we draw the line?" Peggy finally asked, as they kept moving at an energetic pace, scaring off some Sanderlings.

An undulating line of creamy, frothy kelp ash, a byproduct of the seaweed's thick, broad fronds, which had been churned and cooked by the warm summer sea, kept them company as they walked the next two miles. The kelp bloom was flanked by long thin strands of sea grass or cuddled around polished stones. Peggy thought it looked as if someone had squirted whipped cream along the shoreline, and the cream had started to soften. Wispy cirrus clouds floated above without a care in the world.

"I get your point," Cassie said, "but this is a time in my life when I'm seeing my age—from the newest lines in my face that seem so out of place, to the spider veins and cellulite on my legs, to the deeply cracked skin on the heels of my feet.

"I heard that lying on your back reduces wrinkles, but then I remembered reading somewhere that it worsens cataracts."

"Remember that Seurat painting the three of us admired at the museum?" Peggy mused. "Well, we didn't focus on the dots. We stood back and took in the overall effect of the painting. Stop looking in the mirror at each and every line and spot.

"Cassie," Peggy added, "you, of all people, should not be worried about looking your age.

"Don't you remember when you were carded at the organic foods market by a young cashier who did not believe you were eligible for the senior discount? He asked if you were purchasing groceries for your father. Come on, you know you're still a head turner.

"Of course, I don't blame you. We're inundated by ads and commercials telling us the worst sin in life is to look your age. Even some young girls are already using the same anti-aging creams I apply. Cosmetic companies promise to banish crow's feet and wrinkles, but aching knees and stiff backs remind us that we are aging, no matter how youthful we look."

"My mother is still so vain she actually told me to make sure she's wearing a push-up bra at her wake," Barb laughed.

"But you know me. I'm always trying to streamline my life. I need makeup but beyond that, high-maintenance treatments and time-leeching procedures are out. And Botox never did stand a chance—the bacteria would probably turn on me!

"Anyway, a 2011 study found that Botox reduces a person's ability to empathize by erasing the ability to mimic facial expressions.

"I have to admit, though, that a few months ago, I was feeling sorry for myself and missing my former youthful good looks. But I snapped out of it when I watched a story on "20-20" about a teenage girl in Bangladesh on whose face acid had been thrown by a jilted suitor. Her beautiful, young face ruined for life! She would take my aging face in a heartbeat if she could exchange her face for mine. And she would be grateful for it forever," Barb added.

As they skirted around a man and two little boys who were fishing, Peggy noticed that they were casting close in.

"What do you hope to catch today?" she asked.

"Corbina and surf Perch. The Halibut are farther out."

"What are you using for bait?"

"My kids are digging up these tiny sand crabs. See?" He held one up.

As they resumed their previous walking pace, Peggy looked at her friends. "You know what? There are so many other elements that contribute to our overall image—things like posture, how we move and walk, facial expressions, voice and tone, bone structure, and the biggie—attitude. Consider that a woman with a complete makeover can still appear matronly.

"I guess my main concern is that the more we decide to do for our physical appearance now, the more difficult it will be to stop. Dare we assume that we will have the energy and the funds to run back and forth for procedures indefinitely?"

"Right," said Barb. "What happens when the day comes, and it inevitably will (either for financial reasons, health restrictions, or because the skin gives out and can't take any more treatments or procedures), that a woman cannot have her face 'done' anymore? The facial fillers dry up, the implants recede, and the lips shrivel. What then? Will she be able to accept the drastic change in her looks? And what a shock when everything suddenly appears as it really is!"

"Maybe it's better to follow my grandmother's example," Peggy suggested. "In old age, her beautiful facial features were not at all diminished by the patina of delicate lines in her face. Just as the patina of sterling silverware has an attractive look once all the lines and scratches have settled into place, so her facial lines converged over the years into an integrated whole.

"I used to marvel at her total acceptance of the aging process. After all, I wondered, wasn't it extremely difficult for a woman with outstanding beauty to have to give it up? But she seemed to gracefully move forward into every stage of her life. Slowly, steadily, naturally. She adjusted, and we adjusted to her aging. What an example!

"She made the best of whatever she had left and then let her personality take care of the rest. She got up every morning, made herself look as good as she reasonably could within a reasonable period of time—was always clean, neat, and smelled absolutely wonderful—and then got on with her day."

The three of them were quiet for the last few minutes of their walk until they reached the beach parking lot.

"Guess what happened to me on the way back home from Starbucks last Saturday," Cassie asked. As I was doing my daily facial exercises—mouthing exaggerated *a-e-i-o-u's*—while stopped at a red light, I caught a peripheral glimpse of the driver to my right. It was the principal of the school I hope to continue teaching in, unless he now thinks I'm nuts. He was staring at me in wide-eyed shock," Cassie wailed.

"Don't worry about it," Barb and Peggy said, almost in unison, as they tried to muffle their laughter.

While Peggy was sautéing button mushrooms in olive oil that evening, a summary thought flitted through her mind. Be as attractive as you reasonably can and have fun with putting yourself together. It makes you feel good, and it also makes others feel good. The underlying message is *I matter; you matter.*

# 17

*Peggy'sMoments.com*

## WHAT'S YOUR WORST HAIRDRESSER STORY?

### September

One of the most frustrating challenges about moving, at least for a woman, is finding a new hairdresser. It's almost as aggravating as finding a new gyn.

I am convinced that most hairdressers only know how to do about three or four hairstyles, and you are going to come out of their salon with one of those styles. It doesn't matter how much you gesticulate in front of the mirror while explaining what you want, how many magazine pictures you show them, or how much they assure you, again and again, that they understand exactly what you want.

The first hairdresser I tried when Mack and I moved to our present house stared at my shoulder-length hair for a couple of minutes with a pained expression.

"Look at all these split ends," she was finally able to utter. "Your roots are showing, and you're even beginning to grow some nasty stark white hairs in your eyebrows."

"Here's a picture of the kind of hairstyle I'd like," I said, handing it to her.

"Oh, it's you," she smiled. "I'm going to take care of all your problems, just relax."

Two hours later, I left the salon hoping I wouldn't see anyone I knew on the way to my car. I grabbed my sunhat to cover my butchered hair and donned sunglasses to hide my thick, *Groucho Marx*—style, dirty blonde eyebrows.

While waiting for my hair to grow out, I still needed a hair colorist. One of my neighbors recommended someone, and for several months, all went well. Until one day.

"Your ends matched the rest of your hair when you left here last time. I had your hair color even all over and perfect. I remember.

"Now you come back four weeks later and your ends are darker," she said, accusingly. "There is no way your ends could be this dark without something with color pigment in it having been applied to your hair or rinsed through your hair."

She signaled to another stylist to consult about my hair disaster. Finally, after standing over my head of hair and deliberating for several minutes, while referring to hair swatch charts, the other stylist asked me, "Are you taking any medications?"

*Well, I've stopped taking hormones,* I thought, *and that has caused everything else to go haywire, why not just add my strange hair color change to the list!*

My hairdresser was adamant. "Tell me, are you using any special rinse or other product on your hair?"

"I've only been using the shampoo and conditioner I bought from your salon and nothing else," I answered. She clammed up.

To break the awkward silence, I offered, "Well, maybe little aliens are kidnapping me at night and coloring my hair."

No laughter. "In all my years as a colorist, I've never seen anything like this," she retorted.

So you can see why I had to change hairdressers yet again. The new one solved my hair color dilemma during my first visit and immediately started working on my limp crown hair problem.

"I'm adjusting your hair's aura," he assured me in his strong French accent. "Look how happy the hair in your crown is now!"

Now I ask you, can I pick a great hairstylist or what?

## 18

# DECORATIVE SURGERY

*She got her looks from her father. He's a plastic surgeon.*
—Groucho Marx

"One thing I won't do to look better," announced Barb, "I will never ever have cosmetic surgery! Voluntary anesthesia—no way—and elective snipping, slicing, stitching, and suturing—are you kidding?"

"Well, I've got better ways to spend my money than to go under the knife just to achieve a certain look," Cassie chimed in.

"It's not just about the money," said Barb. "A world-famous woman, who would have the *crème de la crème* of plastic surgeons, plus limitless help afterward, has given thumbs down to unnecessary surgery and anesthesia. Her wisdom in this area supersedes any vanity."

"Renoir certainly wouldn't have wanted his models to be liposuctioned." Peggy laughed, as she stopped for a moment to pick up a small pale blue stone that was crystal clear.

"I mean, there's enough pain and risk in life," continued Barb, at a rather high-decibel level. "Why add the stress of decorative surgery to your body? Besides, we all see the faces that are pulled too tight, but many of the really bad endings are kept under wraps.

"I've got an acquaintance who is fond of saying that she'll never get old because she will get a facelift every few years. Right! Are any of the thirty billion neurons in her brain working?" Barb exclaimed.

"You can get your face lifted, your 'twins' lifted, and your natural seat cushion lifted, but you can't stop the aging process. Our internal organs look more dilapidated by the nanosecond, and our backs and knees still ache. No lifting, lowering, tucking, or trimming will change our true age.

"Speaking of breast implants, I read in my nurses' journal that the newest ones require longer incisions and may twist or turn in time, causing the breast to look uneven. Drew says they would look like cross-eyed boobs," Barb chuckled.

A toddler was wobble-running toward the ocean. "Look at you go," Peggy called out, giving a child-like hand wave. Summer would be officially over in a matter of days, but the beaches would still look and feel like summer for some time to come.

"As I was trying to explain," Cassie jumped in, her voice in crescendo mode, "I have to question whether it is right to take even a small risk simply to appear younger or to have a fresher look. It seems to me a frivolous way to spend time, energy, and money. Do I have to look perfect to achieve something of significant value?

"I don't have to be the best-looking woman in the nursing home one day. Then they could put on my tombstone: *She looked young . . . but her body gave out.* If I ever have three thousand dollars to splurge, I'm going to want to contribute it to some cause I believe in."

"Women who sign up for elective surgery need to read the fine print: *Results may vary,*" Barb wanted to add. "Surgeons are not artists, after all.

"Of course, it is understood that there definitely are cases where surgery seems to be necessary—droopy eyelids interfering with your sight, for example. I explained to Drew that an acquaintance of mine would be undergoing surgery to remove loose skin, the result of her impressive weight loss. She was terribly nervous about it.

"'Tell her to make sure the surgeon is an old master rather than a contemporary abstract sculptor,' he quipped."

"So far," Peggy ruminated, "I haven't been tempted to get fat moved from one part of my body to another and, although there's certainly plenty of room for improvement, I haven't succumbed to the slick ads urging me to have my facial skin stretched. At some point, even a rubber band loses its elasticity."

"You've inherited good genes, Peg," said Barb.

"So," Peggy snickered, "I guess I'd better keep an eye on that portrait my father painted of me years ago. You know, the one I keep hanging over the dresser in the bedroom."

"The Portrait of Peggy Conti Crawford," laughed Cassie.

"Still, I don't want to be critical of women who do choose to undergo cosmetic operations," said Peggy. "Constantly barraged with a disproportionate number of ads in women's magazines and TV commercials and infomercials with before and after photos, they make what must be a difficult decision for them. I only hope they're safe, that they achieve the exact look they crave and that their changed appearance helps them feel better about themselves.

"I'm thankful that plastic surgeons can help burn and injury victims," Barb added. "That's necessary and wonderful."

"Exceptions also have to be made for actresses, models, and women on certain other career paths where physical appearance is a major criterion for success. That said . . ." Peggy's voice trailed off.

"The sad thing is that it's becoming as commonplace as going on a picnic," Barb said.

"Well, one good thing that could possibly come out of everyone eventually looking alike is that then women and men would concentrate more on character and personality."

"Seriously, though," Peggy resumed her train of thought, "Mack convinced me long ago that if I started with a facelift, I'd have to keep going with one image repair project after another. He pointed out the impracticality of cosmetic surgery for the purpose of making one part of your body look younger. I can hear him now.

"'Not all of your body parts would match. There would always be some other part of you to do. Let's say someone starts with a facelift. Next, their neck would have to be done, then their hands, and on and on. If you change one thing on your body, you change your total effect—the way all of your characteristics and charms blend together.'"

"Mack's on to something there," chortled Cassie. "I've heard you can even get a *footlift* from some podiatrists so you can fit into your designer shoes."

Later, when Peggy was back home trying to compose a new blog, a startling thought flashed through her mind: *Women have certainly come a long way—we've moved out of the kitchen and into the operating room!*.

She started to type.

# 19

*<u>Peggy'sMoments.com</u>*

## STEPFORD WIVES

Remember how the *Stepford Wives* were all made into look-alikes by their husbands? All the women had enhanced breasts, slim hips, high-powered lips, unfurrowed brows, and bland facial expressions. The men in this old sci-fi movie used Machiavellian methods to stamp out their wives' individuality.

The supreme irony: That's exactly what today's women are doing to themselves—voluntarily. So many women, surprisingly of all ages, are risking their health and sometimes their very lives to attain the currently hyped look. *Women's lib has definitely failed*! Men have got the last laugh on all those women libbers of the seventies and eighties who screamed and screeched that they would fight to the death to be free of male dominance. Men today don't have to lift a finger to get exactly what they want.

We've moved back in time to the Victorian Era, when some wealthy women actually had their lower ribs surgically removed to appear shapely, and it would not shock me at all if the trend to completely redesign our bodies ends up with women of the future going out shopping for new body parts.

So . . . what do we do? How about everything sensible to make the most of what we have in the briefest amount of time and then get on with all the important things we need to accomplish. Our *look* will be a good one if we stay healthy and interested in life and in others. Enthusiasm is catching, and surgery cannot confer that.

Satisfied with her blog, Peggy grabbed her cell phone and called her friends. "There's an end-of-summer special at one of the spas on their *chocolate cake scrubs and pumpkin spice facials.* Between that and surgery—no contest! Want to join me?"

# FALL

*If I could not walk far and fast, I think I would explode and perish.*

—Charles Dickens

# 20

# A CHANCE ENCOUNTER

*You don't know a woman until you have had a letter from her.*
—Ada Leverson (1862-1933)

<u>From: Peggy</u>
<u>To: Barb and Cassie</u>

Dear friends,

Guess whom I met at my alumni reunion in Indiana last Saturday when I had to miss our walk? Trent Leclerc. He's the boyfriend I was pinned to in my senior year of college. Turns out he's been divorced for years and lives in Colorado.

Yesterday morning, he sent a text message letting me know he will be in San Diego next month for a stockholders meeting. He asked if we could have lunch then and catch up on each other's lives. Before one of you asks, yes, he knows I am married. I just think he is being friendly.

*Now for true confessions, I have to admit, though, that I felt mightily drawn to him and old feelings were stirred. The tempting thought that has been flashing through my mind sporadically ever since is:* The window of opportunity is closing for any extracurricular excitement in my life. It's now or never.

*Does this mean I need to jump-start my marriage or something?*

*How I envy your sparkling new romance, Cassie! I don't want to go too gently into that long night. I feel as if I'm grasping at the last straws of my former looks, feelings, passions, hopes, and dreams.*

*A few nights ago, I had a dream about Trent so real that when I woke up, it literally took me two or three minutes to know which was the reality—the dream or my conscious life. In the dream, we were back in college, young again, and he asked me to stay there with him. As I started to come out of my dream state, he screamed out, "No, no, don't go, don't go, you won't be able to get back to me!"*

*Are mankind's dreams the true reality as some Indian tribes believed long ago?*


From: Cassie
To: Peggy
Cc: Barb

*Glad you're back and that you had a good time, Peggy. You were missed.*

*What you are actually craving is attention, and it's terribly addictive. Be on your guard, my friend.*

*You've got what counts with Mack. Think of all the challenges conquered as well as good times you two have shared since you got married after college. You had a choice between Trent and Mack back then, and you chose Mack.*

*What if you ever needed dialysis or chemo? Mack would go through it with you. Would some new thrill stick around for the serious stuff? Get to know Mack again. Reserve some time and just talk and be together. And get to know yourself again too. Sometimes we need to stop doing and take time out to simply Be.*

*As for me, remember the lawyer I thought I was crazy about last year? He aroused primal instincts till the night he blew his nose at the dinner table and then proceeded to cough directly at me. Well, that blew any chance!*

*I am not looking for the kind of constant ecstatic passion that makes women unable to think straight. I want a soul, not just the body that houses it; a romance with just the right mix of passion and fun. Actually, talking with each other and listening, really listening, can give a relationship all the pizzazz it needs.*

*At this point, Nicholas and I are happily discovering common interests, and sometimes we connect as if we had known each other in some long-ago, faraway place. Next date will be to see a play in two weeks. Can't wait! Love is so different now—new qualities to appreciate, new joys.*

*See you soon.*

From: Barb
To: Peggy
Cc: Cassie

*Dear Peggy,*

*I can tell from what you expressed in your e-mail that you've already made up your mind to meet Trent for lunch.*

*Don't you ever get the desire to be pampered? For someone to put your microwaveable heating pad into the oven and then place it gently where it hurts? Well, who would be more likely to do that for you, Trent or Mack? Just ask yourself that.*

*Love you. Te amo.*

## 21

# WEIGHTY CHALLENGES

"How can I have gained three pounds overnight?" Cassie screeched.

"How on earth can a person go to bed at night one weight and get up the next morning weighing more? Why can't I drop three pounds the same way?"

"I've awakened in the morning to a one-inch chin hair and spider veins that weren't there the night before—a lot of strange things can happen while we're sleeping," Barb answered sardonically.

"Cassie, they say those few extra pounds you've got can actually protect you from fractures and increase bone density," Peggy consoled. "But we don't want them!"

"I'll tell you why it's so difficult to drop pounds," said Barb. "Everything's named after food—from my chocolate brown sofa to my caramel floorboards. You go to a spa and every procedure's named after a dessert or candy. You choose paint for your house, and the colors remind you of food. Even clothes have names like cinnamon, honey, and cream."

The three companions strode purposefully up the beach on this first Saturday in October, yet another resplendent day.

"Oh, I didn't tell you yet," continued Barb, "I dropped my membership in the workout center. All I got out of it were pain and germs—pain in my lower back plus tendonitis in my arm from using their machines and germs from breathing in all the viruses circulating in their steam room. On top of this, their classes were always jam-packed, and the instructors moved at breakneck speed.

"So anyway, I've developed my own exercise routine using two-and three-pound free weights and doing lots of different stretches. Of course, exercise doesn't need to always be done all at once. Some days, I can't squeeze in forty-five to sixty consecutive minutes. That's okay. Small chunks of exercise throughout the day also add up.

"Sitting down for too many consecutive hours while working or watching TV isn't good for us. The latest thinking is that we should get up every half hour, or at least every hour, and walk away from our chair for a minute or two. I'm trying to also get in the habit of walking while I'm on the phone.

"But please don't think for a minute that I'm bragging. It's downright hard to maintain the perfect weight at my age," as I also told Drew. 'Not for me, I think I'm underweight,' he retorted. I tilted my head and looked at his ample stomach. 'Well,' he explained, 'I'm 80 percent water, and water doesn't count.'"

Cassie crackled, "I've got to remember that one.

"Speaking of walking, it's one of the easiest and best ways to keep your weight in check, something the three of us just naturally enjoy."

"Right, especially if we keep walking past all the food stores and restaurants," Peggy said. "Oh, and an article in *Writers' Magazine* assured me that writing is not only good for the soul, it's good for the body. I'm thinking, yes, as a blogger, I do have to keep my fingers moving!"

Cassie had some practical advice. "If you dislike the taste of plain water, as I do, try drinking a glass or two of water-juice (add one part juice to three parts water) before each meal to really cut your appetite."

"I recently read that water raises your metabolism by 4 percent," added Barb. "When I told Drew, he quipped, 'Sure, if you drink water all day long, you have to keep running to the bathroom and that's what raises your metabolism.'"

"Drew does have a way of putting everything in perspective," Peggy chuckled, before sharing some of her own dieting tips.

"Out of all the diet plans out there, I'm convinced that *behavioral modification* is the most effective method for changing your relationship to food—food is no longer the boss, you are," she explained.

"It boils down to a couple of basic principles. You decide what and exactly how much you're going to eat, arrange it on your plate while you're still in the kitchen, and then bring your plate to the table. That's it, that's what you're going to eat, nothing else. And if you feel full before your plate is empty, stop eating. In fact, some say to stop when you're about 80 percent full.

"Don't act like the Venus Flytrap, which absorbs its meal and then reopens for a second or even a third helping.

"Never plop a container of food on the table, where you will see it, smell it, and hear its siren song.

"And always sit down at the table, even if you're having only one square of dark chocolate or a handful of nuts. If you crave a snack, formalize the moment. Put a placemat on the table, fold a napkin, and place your snack on a small dish. Allow your brain to register that you are eating your snack for the day. Never eat standing up or moving about. No mindless eating. And please, don't eat in the car.

"Choose your food rather than react to it. Make the foods you want to eat the first you'll reach for by placing them in the front of cabinets and fridge shelves. Even though you know you're tricking yourself, it works.

"We have to get rid of the old mentality that if we eat one potato chip, we have to eat the whole bag. Who has the authority here, the potato chip or you?

"It's a question of replacing bad habits with better ones. In my case, I had to train myself to stop automatically reaching for dessert every single day. As author and speaker Joyce Meyer likes to say, 'God rained manna down from the sky, not Twinkies and cookies.'"

"Is there a twelve-step program for sweet-toothers?" asked Barb.

"We should give ourselves a reward for all our discipline. That's another effective principle," suggested Cassie.

"Sounds good to me. Let's buy a big box of Godiva's," Barb agreed. "I'll eat them as a reward right after I lose these ten extra pounds."

"And I'll eat the chocolates first to give myself incentive," Cassie said. "Then, I'll battle the scale."

"Picture this scene," said Peggy animatedly. "I was grocery shopping one day last week, minding my own business, when a rotund jolly-faced man, who was closely watching me as I scrutinized the eggplants, suddenly struck up a conversation.

"'I used to make the best eggplant concoction ever,' he said. 'You see, I was a chef in my younger days. Now I have a number of conditions that restrict my diet.'

"He then went on to tell me his favorite ethnic signature dishes, pronouncing each recipe name perfectly, whether French, Italian, Greek, or Mexican. With passion and longing, he described in detail how to prepare the 'most incredible' lasagna with ground veal.

"'We really shouldn't be talking like this,' I said, 'I'm on a diet also, and it's no use reminiscing about things we no longer can eat.'

"'Well, we can cheat 20 percent of the time and still be okay,' the retired chef responded. I unobtrusively glanced at his waistline.

"Finally extricating myself from this conversation, I selected two extra large eggplants and, by the time I got to checkout line, I had picked up at least eleven additional items that weren't on my list.

"By gum, I reasoned, if I'm going to cheat 20 percent of the time, I'm going to do so in style!"

# 22

_Peggy'sMoments.com_

## COOKING DINNER AND EACH GUEST IS ON A DIFFERENT DIET

**October**

I'm still recovering from a dinner party I gave a couple of weeks ago to celebrate a friend's birthday.

Both my mother and grandmother, who were regarded in their spheres as culinary wonders, never had to grapple with preparing dinner for six guests, each of whom was on a different diet.

Mom and Gram cooked everything from scratch, it's true, but they only offered one entree, along with several sides they had mastered, and one dessert. They did not ask each guest beforehand what they would or could eat nor did they announce their menu ahead of time. After appetizers, everyone just sat down at the dining room table and ate whatever was served. The only comments I recall were positive.

However, for my dinner, nothing was so straightforward and simple. Since each of my guests, during previous gabathons, had either complained or boasted to me about their dietary restrictions or preferences, I felt compelled to call and courteously ask if my menu would work for them. Their responses, although polite, amounted to a unanimous *no*.

"Actually, since you are so kind to ask, you'll want to know that I've started a new diet. I only eat raw veggies now—that's right—for all three of my meals. I'm purging my system of toxins," said my art teacher from painting class.

I already knew that the birthday girl, a writer I had befriended while writing an investigative piece for a magazine years ago, was on a gluten-free diet. All I had to do was assure her I would make plenty of rice, the only grain she can digest, and that I'd use gluten-free cake mix and frosting for her birthday cake. *Or so, I thought.*

"Pl . . . eeeezz, would you also use gluten-free breadcrumbs on the Weiner Schnitzel, sweetie, and, of course, I won't be indulging in your cappellini." *Of course!*

The two ladies from church were exceedingly sympathetic. The rail-thin one, whom I phoned first, spoke for both of them. "Oh, your menu sounds delightful, you're working much too hard, and you shouldn't worry one minute about us. Jane's doing much better with her LDLs and triglycerides, and my blood pressure's gone down some since I threw away the Morton's salt and started checking every single label for sodium content."

*How would my menu rate with the fifth guest on my list?* I wondered, reaching for an antacid capsule for my own temperamental digestive system.

"Oh, I've got a stomach of steel," my neighbor chortled. "Just don't put peanuts in any form on anything, and I'll be fine. No more allergies I know of, at least not yet." *Whew! This is starting to go better, I dared to believe.*

My remaining guest had a predilection for everything organic and was lactose-intolerant. So I decided to take command and begin our conversation by announcing that all food shopping would be accomplished at the organic foods store and that only soy milk would be used in sauces.

"Thanks so much for calling. You know what?" she asked with a high-pitched voice, "I'm on that new diet Dr. Phil is promoting. Have you heard about it?"

A few minutes later, my cell phone jingled merrily. "Peg," said my sister, trying to calm me, "of course you did the right thing to check on your friends' diets; everybody does that now. Just be sure to use extra-light olive oil, and watch out for preservatives and additives, bad fats, sugar, and you're good to go."

I sat down to write my shopping list, a daunting task. Each dish would be as user-friendly as I could make it without completely ripping up its recipe. Two entrees would be added: baked boneless chicken breasts marinated in orange juice (not okay for acid reflux lady but fine for gluten-free writer) and broiled tilapia (good for practically everyone but not okay for veggie lady). *Not to fret: a large salad, no dressing, would make veggie lady blissfully happy.*

There would be no peanuts to threaten allergy lady, and new diet lady would surely be able to graze on what was fast becoming a smorgasbord.

Finally, I thought about my friend on the low-sodium diet and vowed not to add salt to anything. But everyone else would want salt.

*Now, let's see,* I muttered to myself, *what kind of salt should I put on the table? There's sea salt, kosher salt, rock salt, vegetable salt, herb salt . . .*

## 23

# INDIGESTION QUEENS

"So, Barb, tell us what your doctor said about your frequent heartburn," Peggy was anxious to know as soon as they met by the ocean.

"After being tubed by my gastroenterologist, I emerged from his office with a diagnosis of acid reflux and yet another list of foods to avoid. Want to hear some of them? Chocolate (no more Godiva's!), caffeine, citrus fruits, tomatoes, onions, mint, fats, and spicy dishes, everything yummy," Barb told them. "Even my tiny glass of Cabernet Sauvignon with dinner is out.

"You should see me at the supermarket. I already was watching out for sodium, preservatives, and additives. Now, with my newest digestive ailment, I comb the aisles with notepad and pen, calculating grams and analyzing contents. I'm a restrained lioness, lean and hungry, avidly checking labels. Younger shoppers must think I'm a phobic foodie, but the middle-aged and older customers simply nod and smile."

"What's left for any of us to eat?" whined Cassie. "Even those of us who don't have a specific gastrointestinal issue are mercilessly barraged with dire warnings that anything we like must be bad for us.

"When I was in my twenties, I remember devouring baguettes stuffed with Camembert cheese and sweet butter sold on the streets and everywhere in Paris. That was long ago, when we could enjoy eating what we craved, before we knew the havoc that cholesterol, saturated fats, and sugar wreaked on our digestive systems."

"My worst sin now is sneaking Paul Newman's low-fat, low-sodium popcorn into a movie theater," inserted Peggy.

"Nicholas has an idea for a diet in a box," Cassie resumed. "He would call it the *Air Diet*. The cover of the box would promise: *sodium-, cholesterol-, and fat-free, with no additives, preservatives, artificial ingredients, or calories.* The background picture would be a blue sky. Anytime you were tempted to overeat, you'd open the box and there would be nothing in it," explained Cassie. "But psychologically, you'd feel better . . . so he thinks," she laughed.

Barb picked up where she had left off. "Guess what else? To prevent heartburn, I can't lie down flat for three hours after I eat. So if we have a late dinner, I need to sleep on the recliner until enough time has lapsed. Drew says he's thinking of taking the recliner as an income tax reduction—the chair has become a medical necessity."

"It could be worse," Cassie smiled. "One of my neighbors with severe acid reflux had to raise the head of her bed up on six-inch wood blocks, which makes her bed look like a sliding board."

As someone with a supersensitive, unpredictable digestive tract, it was high time Peggy added her theory to their discussion. "Bad food in the fifties, sixties, and seventies is the reason so many of us now suffer from a variety of digestive challenges.

"The bologna and processed cheese sandwiches, the greasy subs crammed with cold cuts high in saturated fats, the tuna salad swimming in mayo, the greasy hamburgers on bread soft enough to form a ball of yeast in your stomach—this former way of eating is the culprit. As a result, now I'm the indigestion queen!

"Today, a typical loaf of American bread is still as soft as cotton, and fast-food has its devotees; but at least there's an ample availability of bread with a substantial chewy texture as well as an awareness of better food choices," she said.

"There's awareness, and yet, when I was channel-surfing recently," Cassie said, "I happened upon celeb chef Paula Deen's show as she cheerily prepped a hamburger, topped it with a fried egg and bacon, and then sandwiched it in between two honey doughnuts."

"Hard to believe!" Peggy exclaimed.

"Well, some women have digestive systems of steel. That TV show has a large following who would probably like that recipe for a summer backyard party."

"Even some vitamins and supplements can leave us with a heavy, uncomfortable feeling," said Barb. "The latest belief is that multivitamins are a waste of money. They merely produce expensive urine. In these pills, we are swallowing all of the nutrients at the same time and thus creating competition for absorption in our intestines."

"I've found that it's best to eat a wide variety of foods for the trace elements, many of which have not even been identified or named and which are not in supplements," said Peggy.

"My gastro told me the reason I experience so much indigestion is that I'm repressing too much. So now that I've advanced to intermediate Italian lessons, I can yell at Drew in Italian," Barb chuckled.

"*A la faccia di tua zia in carriola!* is one of my favorite expressions for letting him know I have lost my patience."

"Doesn't he get upset?" asked Cassie.

"All the expression means is, 'At the face of your aunt, who is in a wheelbarrow,' if you translate it literally. The Italians have tons of wonderfully imaginative expressions like this one that allow you to really get the satisfaction of telling someone off, without permanently alienating them," Barb explained, popping a berry-flavored, ultrastrength Tum and chewing it slowly.

"Barb, pretty soon you'll know more Italian than I," observed Peggy, "and here I'm the one with the Italian heritage on my father's side. But you are definitely right about using these expressions to release bottled-up tension. That's what my dad used to do."

"Chewing gum is also relaxing, but it causes wrinkling around the lips," Cassie threw in.

"Look, I realize that starving people all over the world would be thrilled with my unlimited supply of fresh fruits and veggies, but I want to complain a little, at least for now, until I make the necessary mental and emotional adjustments to my new diet," Barb continued.

"'An apple a day really does keep the doctor away,' I told Drew one sunny afternoon, as I proudly bit into the nutritious substitute for the slice of chocolate cake I really wanted.

"'Ten apples a day keep your friends away,' he chortled."

"I'm always trying to figure out what to eat and how to make it palatable," inserted Cassie, "so I'm lucky to have Nicholas take over in the kitchen when he gets time. He loves to cook, and one of his best dishes is salmon marinated overnight in lime juice, chives, fennel seeds, and parsley and then broiled."

"For me, breakfast is simple—Kava (an instant coffee that's acid-neutralized), my very own oatmeal concoction, and blueberries on the side," Peggy said. "My oatmeal recipe is a delicious way to lower LDLs while giving me a reason to get up on mornings I'd rather sleep in.

"Just add two tablespoons of sunflower seeds (hulled), one tablespoon of chopped walnuts, one tablespoon of raisins, and one cup of nonfat soymilk to one-fourth cup of Quakers Oats. After heating for a minute-and-a-half in the microwave, sprinkle it with cinnamon.

"And Barb, if you think you can't live without tomato sauce, you've got to try my linguini with extra light olive oil. It's equally satisfying. I cook one clove of garlic, sliced, for a few minutes in the oil, just long enough to flavor the oil. After removing the garlic, I add the oil to the cooked pasta and then top it with one tablespoon of pine nuts, and crumbled, herbed goat cheese," Peggy explained.

"As a side vegetable, I find it therapeutic to slowly pick apart a steamed artichoke while dwelling on the good things that have come my way. My accountant husband loves to crack pistachios open after dinner and then line them up in five rows of six tiny nuts across."

The three women shared a few more of their best recipes and finally had to agree that, despite their dietary restrictions, there were still plenty of tasty dishes just waiting to be created.

"We might as well have fun with the food challenge," Peggy smiled. "Mack knows exactly where to find the freshest and largest radishes, good for his hypertension, and nonfat milk in glass bottles. I have a place for Brazil nuts, plain, no salt, no oil. Once a day is beneficial to the immune system.

"Between the two of us, we easily comb five or six food stores in a two-week period, each of which is best for something. We are amused by friends back in Indiana who shop for everything in only one supermarket; of course, they must think we're the ones who are nutty."

With all their talk about food, Peggy couldn't wait to write her next blog about an experience she and Mack had soldiered through at a trendy restaurant one evening. At least, having to focus her full attention on writing would take her mind off Trent for the remainder of the day. Or would it?

# 24

_Peggy'sMoments.com_

## WAITER, BRING BACK MY PLATE!

### Third Saturday in October

If you want to have a relaxed dinner in a good restaurant, be on your guard. They might clear your table before you've finished eating.

Have you ever had your plate whisked out from under your chin while you're still eating? Flash-frozen in my memory is our experience at a trendy seafood restaurant. My husband was only about halfway through his entree when he laid down his fork so he could refill our wine glasses. Big mistake! At that exact moment, my own fork happened to be poised in midair, aimed squarely at my mouth, with my last jumbo shrimp scampi secured in its tines.

Suddenly, our waiter lurched out of nowhere and swept my plate out from under me (and my airborne shrimp), then grabbed Mack's dish, upon which still lay several broiled scallops and a partly eaten baked potato. "Would you like to see the dessert menu," he asked innocently.

"Not until I finish my dinner," Mack responded drolly.

"But, sir, you put your fork down. I thought you were done."

"Well, my wife's fork was still up in the air," harrumphed my husband.

Chewing my shrimp while watching this little scene unfold, I made a quick mental note: *Do not, for any reason, put your fork down until you are ready to relinquish your dinner plate, not even to give your digestive tract a rest. Keep the utensil in your hand and wave it around a bit while you talk so the waiter will perceive it as still "in action."*

Then there was the sumptuous brunch at a five-star hotel to celebrate my birthday. Picture this: Mack's plate of pancakes was directly in front of him while his second plate of melon slices, pineapple chunks, and assorted berries was to his right. He ate only two of the cantaloupe slices and then happily attacked his pancakes.

Without any warning, a complacent busboy, who had been refilling our coffee cups, came up from behind our table and swooped down on Mack's fruit plate. As he rushed the plate, still laden with fruit, back toward the kitchen, he called over his shoulder, "Let me get this out of your way, sir."

Mack calmly got up, walked over to the buffet table, and filled a new plate with fruit.

Next, it was my turn to protect my plate. It could disappear in a flash. Bending slightly forward, I hovered over my Belgian waffles while also holding onto my dish with my left hand so the waiter would have to walk around to the front of our table and face me in order to try to nab my waffles. At least, he could not sneak up on me.

"Can I take your plate?" the obsessed waiter asked at regular intervals during the course of my meal. *Could it possibly be that they need to make room for other customers?* I wondered. Glancing around, I noted a few empty tables were still available.

By the fourth time the question was put to me, I had had enough and became defensive. "You can, but you'd better not," I snapped. The other customers looked at me. "No one's getting my plate!"

"But you've finished eating, ma'am," the waiter proclaimed.

"Do you see those three blueberries on the dish? Well, I still intend to eat them," I said, guiltily pondering whether the restaurant was short of dishes.

Two minutes later, a woman in a navy suit strode over to our table. "I understand you're not finding things very satisfactory here," she said. "As the manager, I'd like to know if there's anything I can do."

"Everyone wants my plate. They have wanted it from the first moment I started eating," I informed her. The manager looked at me as though I were mentally challenged. Mack and I left, heads held high, never to return.

Gone are the days when properly trained servers actually would wait for the standard signal . . . fork and knife lying side by side across the plate. Now they race to your table like the pale rider of the Apocalypse every ten minutes to ask, "How's your dinner? You still working on it?"

I still enjoy eating out, but my rule of thumb is to get a firm grip on my plate if, by chance, I must turn my head away from it to sneeze or say hello to someone.

# 25

# FIRST LOVE

*From: Peggy*
*To: Barb and Cassie*

*Dear friends,*

*Before I call it a night, I just had to slip into the study and e-mail you both about my incredible get-together with Trent for lunch today in the Gas Lamp Quarter. We talked for two hours straight about our college experiences and about what each of us has been doing since. Then Trent headed back to the afternoon session of his stockholders' meeting, and I drove home.*

*We spoke as if we had simply picked up where we left off a lifetime ago. The decades in between dissolved, they no longer existed. Trent is the one who taught me how to dance the Twist (Remember the sixties hit, "Twist and Shout?") and the Pony, the one I sat next to at college football games,* the one I crammed for exams with, and the first man to ask me to spend the rest of my life with him.

He's handed his advertising agency over to his son to run; now, he does some part-time financial investment consulting. When his marriage fell apart, he bought a condo in Colorado, and he divides his time between there and his Indiana townhouse.

But Barb, you were right that I should have been on my guard. Feelings I had back in prehistoric times were reignited. I am in semi-shock about the eruption of a passionate longing I never dreamed would happen again for me, not in this lifetime.

As we oh-so-slowly walked out of the restaurant, Trent said he hoped we'd meet again sometime soon. The he said he would be flying out in the morning. In unspoken words, as we lingered in the parking lot, he was really leaving the next move up to me. I was rooted to the spot. At that very moment, it started to rain (which had to happen sooner or later in southern CA after a six-month dry period). How do I want to spend the rest of this afternoon? I asked myself.

Somewhere deep inside me the decision was made. "We'd better make a run for our cars," I blurted out, as the raindrops thickened. "Have a safe trip back."

Now what? Anything? Should I e-mail Trent, thanking him for lunch? Should I tell him how much I enjoyed catching up on each other's lives? Or do I just let this whole thing go?

From: Barb
To: Peggy
Cc: Cassie

*Okay, Peggy, we have really got to talk. First off, you already thanked Trent in person for lunch and told him you enjoyed sharing. Think about starting a correspondence with him. Now, ask yourself: For what purpose? Where would this lead? Then what?*

*It always comes down to switching. In a future relationship with Trent, you would be exchanging one set of annoyances for a different set of little everyday habits that can agitate you as much as Mack's. You can't expect one person to fulfill every single one of your needs. And passion, or being "in love," is never enough. Never has been, never will be.*

*In the heat of passion, we can accept people into our lives we ordinarily would not give the time of day to. You really do not know Trent now; you only know the Trent who used to be—in a different place, in a different time, under different circumstances. Whom has he evolved into?*

*What do you really know about the sixty-something Trent? How does he eat? Does he robotically chomp through his meal or does he savor each morsel? How does he act when he has a cold or hears bad news or is under extreme pressure?*

*I remember seeing a rerun of an old* Father Knows Best *TV episode where Betty spends her summer vacation on a ranch and "falls in love" with a young cowboy. She is absolutely lovesick when she returns home. But a few months later, when the cowboy comes to visit Betty on her turf, he completely turns her off by his inability to adapt to her lifestyle and to fit in with her friends.*

*Peggy, the way you (and I too!) worry about germs, all you have to do is to think of all the bacteria on Trent's lips. Then you won't want to kiss him* **soooo** *much.*

*Pensa alla salute. Think of your health.*


<u>From: Cassie</u>
<u>To: Peggy</u>
<u>Cc: Barb</u>

*I'm e-mailing while the chicken's broiling, so I'll have to keep this short.*

*Somebody wise once said it's not the going to bed with each other at night, which I'm sure would be terribly exciting, but the getting up together in the morning and dealing with all the wonderful/miserable things of the day that matters.*

*What you've got here is the known versus the unknown. You and your husband have a proven track record of dealing with life's myriad twists and turns. You have an intimate comfort with Mack. Schedule in some fun time with him.*

*Have you seen the TV commercial that goes, "We've got fifteen ways to serve some passion with Uncle Ben's rice?"*

*Go get some rice.*

## 26

# STUFF

"I am fed up with shifting, moving, storing, maintaining, organizing, and reorganizing all the superfluous stuff in my house," Barb announced. "I've given my stuff too much power, and I'm about to take it back."

"Well, there are plenty of books that provide step-by-step methods for sorting through your clutter and deciding whether to give it away, sell it, or dump it," Cassie quickly offered.

"Decluttering is doable," Peggy agreed, "and stuff like Mack's should definitely go. But getting rid of precious items to which you are emotionally attached can be heart-wrenching and even impossible for some of us.

"My mom suffered so much emotionally back when she and Dad decided to move to a retirement complex, where there would be no room for the cherished belongings she had collected over a lifetime, things associated with precious family celebrations, objects that jogged memories of trips, vacations, and friendships forged.

"As she explained it to me at the time, her choices in furniture, art objects, accessories, and paintings, as well as in their exact placement, were an expression of her ordered thoughts and beliefs. Over the years, these possessions had absorbed her emotions and spirit and had become an extension of herself. She would look at her dining room table and remember loving moments.

"After she finally moved, she told me she had given away all of her tangible connections to who she was and is, to her life experiences thus far."

It was the first Saturday in November. As if nature had staged a set design as the perfect backdrop for the topic *du jour*, chips and broken chunks of shells were spread across the moist sand, from where the sea had receded hours ago, all the way down to the waterline.

"Hearing about your mom," said Barb, "I am more convinced than ever that this is the time for each of us to start the process of simplifying, of letting go of our accumulations stage by stage, while we still have the nerve to do it. It's too traumatic to have to give it all away in one fell swoop when we're older.

"What we've really got to do is go through our houses, room by room, and classify all of the stuff that has sneakily wrested control of our lives and somehow fused with our identities. Then, we can pull one item at a time from each classification."

"Right," Peggy said, with a slight edge of exasperation. "What am I supposed to do with the linen tablecloths and napkins crocheted by my grandmother? What about the china, silver, and crystal glassware my mom passed down to me because she couldn't say goodbye to them? What do you suggest I do with the spectacular oil paintings my father gave me that were extensions of his personality? Am I to let go of these also?"

Neither of her friends could answer the unanswerable.

"At the other end of the spectrum," Cassie threw in, "the Mongolians are able to pack and unpack all of their belongings in less than two hours."

"That's because they don't accumulate," Barb said. "We, on the other hand, turn our houses into universes of significance by infusing meaning and connection into our assorted souvenirs."

Peggy resumed her rant. "My photo albums will be with me till death do us part! I don't care how many articles are out there telling us how to sort through our meaningful possessions and how great we'll feel after we do it."

"But how many times do any of us actually make it a point to review our old photos? And who's going to look at them when we're gone?" wondered Cassie.

"We really should question each item that we are saving. I haven't touched my ukulele for two years. One more year on the shelf untouched and, I'm going to give it away. I pitched old love letters and journals I wouldn't want my grandchildren to ever read. And no more keepsakes! If I receive one as a present, I will either return it to the store or give it away."

Barb had the last word. "In a book I read many years ago, called *A Home for the Soul*, the author wrote, 'I hope that the rooms and furnishings that surround you become active participants in a life of vitality, depth, and meaning, an environment where your spirit can thrive.'

"When I read this passage to Drew, he said, 'Yeah. The furniture will become an active participant if you move it.'"

By the time Peggy arrived back home, after stopping to buy a salad mix of baby kale and other greens, plus running two more errands, she was ready to pour out her frustration about all of Mack's accumulated, meaningless stuff. *Yes, Mack's stuff has got to go*, she told herself. While he was occupied with installing a new kitchen faucet, she typed the heading of her next blog: "Living with a Paper Packrat."

# 27

*Peggy'sMoments.com*

## LIVING WITH A PAPER PACKRAT

### November

Against formidable odds, I am determined to declutter my house.

It is difficult enough, I admit, to part with some of my own sentimental things, but trying to get rid of Mack's excess stuff is much more challenging. My otherwise lovable packrat husband amasses and squirrels away paperwork and office supplies faster than I can shovel them out.

Piles and piles of unsorted papers, unread magazines, newspaper clippings, junk mail, old bank statements, college and grad school notebooks, e-mails and other computer printouts on a wide range of subjects—all in disarray—clutter the desk and tops of file cabinets in the study. He's also accumulated enough stationery supplies to open a small shop.

If I don't constantly clear his papers, they have a way of invading every single flat surface all over the house. When I complain, he smiles and says, "Wherever I am, that's where my desk is." The only upside is that when I'm searching for something of my own, I know for certain it has not been thrown out.

In the garage, he's got three toolboxes that haven't been opened since before our last two moves (he bought brand-new tools when we moved here), plus garden supplies that will never touch soil or flower. Cardboard boxes that haven't been opened for nine years line one wall of the garage.

*Dare I open them?* I asked myself the other day, bravely venturing into the garage. The first few boxes revealed old pamphlets and brochures from doctors' offices, endless pads of paper with notes taken while watching the History Channel or Suze Orman, maps of places we've never been, and unlabeled video cassette tapes.

Right there and then, I fantasized about simply grabbing everything and dumping it into a giant paper shredder. Ahhh, the wonderful humming sound that would make! I also summoned up my dream of truck after truck pulling up in front of the house to haul away every unusable item.

Alas, I knew that fantasy and dreams do not mesh with the hard reality that I will only be able to eliminate my husband's stuff with the utmost care and patience.

My hair colorist told me she is forced to painstakingly sort through all of her husband's junk, one item at a time, because of possible hidden treasures that might be buried among the debris. This is the direct consequence of what happened one day when she was ready to ditch a foot-high stack of old newspapers that looked a little lumpy. In between the papers, she found a chunk of broken, disintegrating rock, which she placed into a plastic baggie in order to confront him with his sloppiness. But immediately, he knew what it was and cried out, "Oh, that's my grandpa's headstone!"

Peeking inside the garage every once in a while, Mack enjoyed telling me, "Remember, hon, every time you throw out some of my stuff, you're throwing out a part of my spirit too."

I refused to be guilted. Instead, I pictured my dear one joining a *Stuff Anonymous* group and standing before them confessing, "Hello, my name is Mack and I like stuff."

"It's time to streamline and simplify," I announced, when I finally went back inside after a frustrating two hours of work. "If you go first, I'm going to put all your disorganized papers into your coffin so you can spend eternity sorting them out."

Mack only looked at me wryly and said, "That's good, but don't forget the body!"

All the books on decluttering make it sound so straightforward to simply throw away or give away unneeded items, but they don't know I'm dealing with someone whose piles of papers have merged with his being.

His stuff has too much power, I think, remembering my recent discussion with Barb, and he never will take the initiative to part with any of it. I know what needs to go, but how on earth am I going to get the stuff out of here?

Embedded in my memory is the day he actually went running after the city garbage truck convinced I had just then thrown out a box of his old college accounting books. "Wait, wait," he cried, "you can't take that!" (Actually, I already had donated them to a university.)

Sometimes, I catch him opening the trash cans and undoing the plastic trash bags just before our garbage is to be picked up to make sure I haven't snuck something inside one of them. Some kind of sixth or seventh sense is activated and he knows, he just knows, as he gleefully retrieves something or other that he can't possibly live without.

"Your paper cups, plastic tops, and little wood stirring sticks are all over the house, not just on the kitchen counter," I ranted one time. "They're on the coffee tables, in the bathroom, in the garage, and . . ."

"That shows you that I'm moving around; I'm not a couch potato," quipped Mack.

He then reminded me of the day those sticks came in handy at a gas station when a frantic lady could not get her gas tank open. Mack flipped it open with one of the sticks. "There are multiple uses for all my collections," he proudly stated, and I thought about the stack of empty ice cream containers (washed and dried, of course) he uses as "a neat way to dispose of the moist coffee grounds post brewing."

I often reminisce about the marvelous arrangement I had in a previous neighborhood for getting rid of his excessive accumulations without his knowing it. My method was to remove papers and junk from his piles little by little, stuffing them into a thirty-gallon trash bag I kept inside my car trunk. Then, on trash collection day, I'd carry the bulging bag up to my next-door neighbor's curb to mingle with her trash cans. She was very understanding.

History is about to repeat itself. I'm signing off now and heading for the kitchen. I bet my new neighbor would love some homemade cookies.

# 28

# LETTER FROM TRENT

*From: Peggy*
*To: Cassie and Barb*

*Dear friends,*

*Below is a copy of the e-mail letter I just received from Trent. It has knocked the breath out of me. I am filled with a sense of longing. Now what'll I do???*

Dear Peggy,

In the whole observable cosmos, there are billions of galaxies. In each galaxy, hundreds of billions of stars, threaded with clouds of gas and dust, dance and shine in an area of space hundreds of thousands of light-years across.

What are the odds that one man on one small planet, who loved and lost so many years ago, could meet the lady of his dreams again?

Ever since we got together last week, I have been preoccupied with thoughts of you.

Please let me know when you are planning to fly out to see your mother so that I can arrange to be in Indianapolis at the same time. My son is doing an excellent job managing every aspect of my ad agency which frees me up to spend most of my time in Colorado. Still, I do get to Indy every couple of months to do some brainstorming with him and enjoy his company. Of course, the townhouse is always there just waiting for me. It's comfortable and spacious, and I think you will like it as well. We can make two quick stops (to the agency and my place) so I can show you everything, and then we can go out for dinner at a great new restaurant in Carmel or anywhere else you wish.

Waiting for your answer,

Trent


*From: Barb*
*To: Peggy*
*Cc: Cassie*

*Remember when we talked about all the annoying changes in our lives and you mentioned the comeback of some of your old menopausal symptoms like mood swings and raw nerves at times?*

*Your body is still adjusting to being without your hormone pills. I think this is at least part of the reason you have been feeling so restless this year. A free-floating, generalized anxiety is an unpleasant burden and can make a woman much more vulnerable than she normally would be.*

*Taking off my nurse's cap, I want to just say, as your friend, that temptation can exert an irresistible pull. Close that door and don't walk through.*

*Ciao.*


<u>From: Cassie</u>
<u>To: Peggy</u>
<u>Cc: Barb</u>

*Wow! Can Trent write or what? His words would stir a statue of stone to emotion.*

*Delete it and get on with your day. You can't live on words alone.*

*See you Saturday.*

# 29

# FASHION CHALLENGES

"What on earth am I going to wear to Drew's alumni reunion?" Barb wanted to know. "It's going to be a Christmas party in a private home, dressy, but not formal."

It was three o'clock and sixty-four degrees on a typically gorgeous mid-December afternoon. The tide was lazily receding toward its lowest level, which would occur in about an hour. In some sections of the beach, the khaki sand was interspersed with gray-black smudges that made it look as if tractor tires had traversed it recently. Large brown patches of floating seaweed caught Peggy's eye as she glanced toward the ocean.

"I wasted an entire day yesterday trying on outfit after outfit in front of a three-way mirror, under florescent lights, in an overheated department store. Demoralizing and exhausting!

"I'll just bet the famous Margaret Mead never looked in a three-way mirror when she bragged about her 'postmenopausal zest.'"

"You didn't find any possibilities the entire day?" Peggy asked.

"So many of the clothes available now are either too young or too old," Barb said with frustration. "It's as if all the fifty-, sixty-, and seventy-somethings have dropped into a fashion black hole!"

"You're right!" Cassie piped in. "Someone has to clue Madison Avenue in to the fact that we don't want to look like we're on the prowl, but neither do we want to look as matronly as our grandmothers did when they were our age. A definite gap exists for us in-betweeners who need dresses, skirts and tops with class and sophistication in a reasonable price range.

"We are not ready for an elderly look, and we may never be. But at the same time, you don't see anyone of our vintage sashaying down the Paris or New York runways, posing in ads or dazzling us in TV commercials for fashion apparel, do you?"

"Another thing," Barb added, flying off on a tangent of her own. "How often are we the glamorous heroines of any novel or movie? And if we are, we either must have a young costar in the story with us or we must undergo intermittent flashbacks of our earlier days."

"But you know what, ever so slowly, I do think movies will start to feature older women," said Cassie. "I read in a magazine that actress Isabella Rossellini tackles the golden years in her latest film, *Late Bloomers*."

"As far as fashion, though, we're not exactly in any designer's exclusive market niche," Peggy agreed with Barb. "That's okay. As our numbers swell, with more and more of us aging, there will eventually be a rebellion. We'll just shop our own closets and stop buying. Then they'll listen."

"Actually, many of the clothes we already own need only some minor tweaking. I even found a blouse and pants with tags still on them and was guilt-tripped by thoughts of women dying with closets full of outfits they were saving for some unknown future time."

"The trouble with your idea," Cassie said wryly, "is that I've got three sizes of clothes in my closet, two of which I probably will never be able to fit into again."

"So what should I wear?" Barb moaned again, bringing us back to her current puzzle. "Where, oh, where can I find a dress that is not too short, not too clingy, and that actually has some sleeves? Something classy and glamorous?"

"You can always pair a sequined tee with one of those dreadful skirts that make you wonder if all the fashion designers have secretly gotten together to plot which one of them can market the most hideous prints and color combinations," Peggy said facetiously.

"The fashionistas could learn something about design from the Caribbean Reef Squid," she chortled. "These creatures have some thirty-five patterns in their wardrobes with varying colors which they change to suit the particular conditions they find themselves in."

"I recently saw an ad for jiggle-stopping fabrics," smiled Barb. "Now that's something I can relate to."

"All this talk about current fashion challenges has got me reminiscing," said Cassie. "Way back when they were in style, I wore black patent leather boots with miniskirts and black fishnet stockings. This is all back! Even appliquéd jeans are back, to which I say, if you've already worn a current trend once in your lifetime, pass the torch.

"I remember when the 'slut look' was first introduced as an actual style, and no one at that time believed it would last. Amazingly, skin-tight pants and extremely low-cut tops have been successfully mainstreamed by some lucky designers much to the distraction of teenage boys."

"A lot of underwear is now outerwear—lingerie like lacey camisoles and slips," inserted Barb.

"I will give the designers credit for body-shaping jeans and pants in every single length," Cassie decided.

"I'm surprised spike heels are back with all the publicity about super high heels being bad for a woman's back, knees, feet, and posture," Peggy said. "My mother wore two-to three-inch heels till she was eighty-eight, and they were taken away from her. But she would have been risking her life by wearing the five-to six-inch platform stilettos that are being promoted right now."

"The platform part of my dressy heels ranges from one-half to three-quarters of an inch. That's enough to give me a current look without calling more attention to my shoes than to my eyes," Barb said.

"You know something ironical? Peggy went on. "In the upside-down world of fashion, skin-tight tops are stylish for pregnant women while the rest of us, the nonpregnant, are expected to wear the long, loose, shapeless tops."

"I'm dealing with the tees and jersey tops that have no waistline by gathering the fabric at one side until it looks as if I have a waistline and then pinning on a broach to secure the gathered material," Cassie interjected.

Peggy was reminded of her thick wool, navy blue sweater-jacket from college days, which she realized she would never have the heart to give away. Back then, it was trendy to push in the sweater's round, popped-out brass buttons with your thumb. Similar sweaters become popular about every five years or so but not with the same kind of buttons. *Sometimes I get a futuristic vision of myself as the proverbial old lady in tennis shoes, and I'm wearing my college sweater*, she thought.

About ten yards ahead of her, a tall lanky fisherman was frowning. Peggy stopped to ask what he was catching.

"Nothing. See all this eel grass?" he said, casting a disparaging look at it. "That's a sign I should be moving from this spot." Clumps of the thick coarse eel grass contrasted sharply with the slender, graceful swirls of sea grass they had passed by earlier.

"Look, Barb," Peggy finally said, "you have time before your event. Why don't you pick out some beautiful fabric and just go and get a dress made, something that makes the most of your assets and the least of everything else. The wrap dress has been described as the fashion world's sweetest gift to grown-up women. You can play it up or down, wear it day or night.

"But make sure you choose a fabric that is washable so you never have to take it to the cleaners," she advised emphatically.

"I found a stunning silk and linen-blend top with embroidery along its V-neckline on sale last month and wore it out to dinner with several friends where it got accidentally splashed with red wine. Everyone said the spots would come out, don't worry.

"The cleaners said they might not. I nervously left my top there and waited a week before calling to check. 'We're working on it,' they said. 'Should I be worried?' I asked.

"Two weeks passed and the phone rang. 'We can't seem to find your top,' they told me, 'our new girl forgot to enter it into the computer and it could be almost anywhere. But don't worry, you will come out ahead.'

"'No, I won't,' I answered dryly, 'I bought it on sale, and I will never find a replacement top as beautiful that is also on sale for half price.'"

"Don't get me started about cleaners," Cassie said.

"I was so concerned about what to wear and, thanks to you two, my problem is solved," smiled Barb. "Now I need to concentrate on Drew.

"I can't even get him into the men's department at Nordstrom's. I practically had to drag him kicking and screaming to the store last week. As we walked toward the men's department, his pace slowed noticeably. He suddenly stopped short at the outer edge of men's clothing, looked deeply into the section, turning his head to the right and to the left, and then said, 'Okay, I told you they wouldn't have anything. Let's go.'

"Can you believe it? He never even walked into the men's department!"

As the three of them laughed, Cassie undid the sweater that was wrapped around her waist and draped it over her shoulders. It was almost four-thirty, and the temperature had dropped a few degrees while they were walking.

"So . . . ," she began, turning to look at Peggy, "before we leave, I have to ask, what's the latest with Trent?"

"I never imagined being torn between two men, who could not be more different from each other, at this time in my life. This whole thing has caught me off guard."

"Temptation always does. I hope you'll at least consider letting it go," said Cassie.

"I'm considering both possibilities."

"Are you planning to write or to call him back with your answer," Barb wanted to know.

"At this point, I have no idea. But thank you both so much for walking through this with me."

# 30

# NICHOLAS ALMOST PROPOSES

*From: Cassie*
*To: Peggy, Barb*

I couldn't wait another week to tell you both—Nicholas proposed, or at least he attempted to. I brushed it off and abruptly changed the subject. And that was that.

It happened a couple of days after our walk. He had taken me out for a late dinner right after line dancing class, and we just about had finished eating.

"Cassie," he began, "I think you know that one of the best days of my life was the day you grapevined right into my open arms. I sensed even then that there would come a time I would wrap them around you and ask you a life-changing question."

Before he could continue, I said, as casually as possible, "Nicholas, I love you too, but I've got an extra early morning tomorrow with dozens of ungraded papers still to do."

Later, I lay in bed trying to analyze my reaction. Nicholas is simpatico, but I missed out on all the previous years with him, and I don't just want his older years. I enjoy seeing him, but I'm afraid to commit to living with him every single day.

I had to ask myself what kind of fool I am to be so afraid of all the unknowns in a committed relationship. How can I be so sure that staying single will mean a smooth path ahead?

Even so, I finally drifted off to sleep promising myself to stay unattached.


<u>From: Peggy</u>
<u>To: Cassie</u>
<u>Cc: Barb</u>

Cassie,

Your first husband behaved badly, so you are afraid history could repeat itself. You're just plain scared to give yourself completely again.

I also think you don't want to face the possibility of having to care for Nicholas, should his health ever decline severely down the line.

I have come to the conclusion that almost everything we decide to do or not do poses a risk. Business guru Jim

*Collins says he has no more emotion about uncertainty than he does about gravity. His books are requested frequently at the library so I copied down one of his quotes for you: "Gravity just is. I don't wake up in the morning afraid of gravity. You've got to learn how to live with gravity; you've got to learn how to live with uncertainty. The beauty of it is, you can. Successfully, and in very practical ways."*

<u>From: Barb</u>
<u>To: Cassie</u>
<u>Cc: Peggy</u>

*Hi Cassie,*

*Take the risk. At least you'll have company along the way.*

*Seriously, whatever you decide, I'm with you one hundred percent.*

*Ciao.*

# 31

<u>Peggy'sMoments.com</u>

## BEACH LESSONS

### November

I should have worn my hat today at the beach.

Early this morning, I was greeted by a low tide, overcast sky, and only a few vacationers. *Good*, I thought, *I won't even need my hat*; *my zinc sun lotion is more than enough protection for my face.*

So . . . I happily started my routine of fast walking, interspersed with some arm and leg exercises. After some thirty minutes, I was completely relaxed, my mind absorbed by the sights and sounds of the beach: a canopy of stratus clouds over grayish-green water, receding wavelets revealing sand patterns that looked like a quilted bedspread, a few surfers, a kayak, kelp bulbs that popped under my weight, and the plaintive cries of seagulls. All was right with the world.

And then, I looked up at a couple of Blue Herons flying directly over my head.

*Splat!*

I really should have worn my hat today at the beach.

# 32

# PET PEEVES

*Where shall I begin? Which of all my important nothings shall I tell you first?*
—Jane Austen to her sister Cassandra

The first Saturday in December, Peggy and her friends chose to meet at Seagrove Park, one of two coastal parks in Del Mar adjacent to the beach.

"Driving down here, I was passed by so many drivers going eighty miles an hour or more on the I-5. I would just love to own a small army tank so I could fearlessly take them on. What an aggravation!" Barb exclaimed. "This is definitely one of my pet peeves."

"Oh, I've got some great ones," volunteered Cassie. "You're at a cocktail party and someone's spit lands on your cheek. Should you wipe it off or let it sink in?

"Another guest at the same party double-dips into the crab fondue you were dying to taste. As if that's not enough, the waiter handles the forks by their tines as he lays them on the table.

"These are just a few of my pet peeves; I've got lots more," she said.

"Unflushed toilets in ladies'rooms, trash left on the beaches, sweaty handshakes . . ."

"Then there are the daily calls from telemarketers even though you're on the National Do Not Call List," Barb snapped, "junk e-mail you must wade through, and all the snail mail you have to take time out to shred because of possible identity theft. Gone are the days when you could simply scoop up all the junk mail and dump it the trash can.

"How about dealing on the phone with these prerecorded menu lists? After you wade through several submenus and get to the third tier of menus, do not lose patience and yell at the robotic voice. If you do, it will say, 'I don't understand' and take you all the way back to the main menu.

"And have you ever tried to settle a complicated billing issue and been connected to a rep in India with an extremely heavy accent?" she asked.

"So this is our topic today?" asked Peggy, as she admired the well-maintained houses that lined the Del Mar beach.

Cassie was fired up and resumed ticking off her pet peeves. "The most ridiculous line used in so many movies today is the '*Are you okay?*' question. It is always asked of someone who's been through some ghastly ordeal and is black and blue all over. For once, I'd like the victim to answer, '*No.*'

"Then there's the current use of i.e. while speaking. Let's keep i.e. on paper, please."

"Speaking of movies," Peggy interjected, now fully engaged in their topic, "foul words are spewed from different characters as their one and only way of expressing their emotions. Their vocabulary does not extend beyond a few constantly repeated vulgarities and curse words. And some screenwriters today even seek an excuse to plop someone who has a fetish into their crude comedies, someone who has nothing at all to do with the plot. Original films are so superior to their remakes. Case in point: the 1936, *Mr. Deeds Goes to Town.*

"Old detective movies and TV shows had intricate plots and intriguing dialogue. Now, they principally feature chase scenes, destruction, computerized visual effects, and explicitly brutal murder scenes. The little bit of dialogue, interspersed here and there, is on an eighth-grade level at best."

"And for the romantic scenes, they used to just close the bedroom door. Now, the movies are making voyeurs out of all of us," added Barb.

"Obviously," Cassie added, "true journalism is dead. A big pet peeve with me is that hearsay and made-up quotes are publicized in newspapers as if they are facts. And both sides of an issue are rarely presented."

The friends walked in silence for a few minutes, absorbing each other's concerns, and then Barb spoke up again.

"One of the best places to get sick if you're not already, is in a doctor's waiting room, what with everyone there coughing and sneezing in an enclosed space. Another place to catch a bug is at a sandwich shop, where the sandwich maker, sans gloves, doubles as the money-handling cashier."

"Right," Peggy agreed, "you can also get sick from your own medications. Cure one thing, get another. It's a switcheroo of one set of symptoms for another. Any pill you take might provide relief from your particular ailment while setting you up for side effects much worse that your original condition.

"For years, doctors and others aggressively urged us to take calcium for our aging bones. Now, we're informed that calcium can cause heart problems.

"Did you know it's estimated that 20 to 30 percent of all medications, tests, and procedures are unnecessary?

"Everything in life's a quid pro quo. If you park in the shade, your car stays cool. Then you come back and your car is covered with bird droppings.

"There's some new drug being advertised on TV for social interaction disorder. The list of possible side effects includes diarrhea, flatulence, and nausea. So the patient would no longer be afraid to socialize, but who on earth would want to be with her?" Peggy had to laugh at her own examples.

"Can you believe that when Mack's elbow flared up to the size of an egg from bursitis a few years ago while we were out of town, an emergency room doctor actually suggested removing the bursa?"

"Sure," said Barb. "Years ago, a podiatrist wanted to remove three of my toenails, saying the fungus in them would never go away. Long story short, I subsequently saw a dermatologist whose treatment worked, and I kept my nails."

On the way home, Peggy stopped at Cardiff Beach for a chocolate acai smoothie, then proceeded north along the coastal highway. Back home, she swung into her driveway and hesitated while pressing her garage door opener. From the side view mirror, she clearly saw a large dog approaching her front yard. The dog lifted his hind leg, way up high, over her beautiful azaleas. Its owner merely looked on, expressionless, and said nothing. Silently, she added this kind of affront to her list of pet peeves.

As soon as she sat down in front of the computer to compose her next blog, one of her verbal pet peeves flashed across her mind. It was the phrase, "you guys," an expression that also ticked off many of the women Peggy knew and loved.

This seemingly benign phrase has become so common that it is not even noticeable to those who use it, she realized. *Even feminists, who insist upon the use of "he or she" instead of "he" appear to accept this expression. Why?*

*What would be the reaction if we called a group of men "you gals?"*

*This is one of the best examples of how a phrase can insert itself into our language, reach a tipping point, and then take over and actually become part of the daily vernacular. Its widespread usage drives me to distraction, and it begs to be written about.*

*Well, here goes. It's too late to fight it, but at least I'll get it out of my system for once and for all,* she calculated.

*I know, I know, it's become a meaningless salutation, not meant to be taken literally. Most of the time, I ignore it. It's just that I wonder how much farther its usage will go.*

# 33

*Peggy'sMoments.com*

## THE "YOU GUYS" EXPRESSION

### December

Calling everyone "you guys" has gotten out of hand. It doesn't matter if you're young or old, male or female, a parent, or even a grandparent. Everyone is a guy.

It not only annoys me that this expression has completely taken over our vernacular to such an extreme extent, but it intrigues me as well.

The expression "you guys" was actually movie actor James Cagney's signature expression in his popular old gangster movies, which are still shown on cable TV. A sinister, sneering Cagney would always give orders to his thugs, starting with "Okay, you guys."

This designation slipped into our everyday language over a decade ago. But why didn't it get old? Why has it spread to this degree? How far will it go? Is the first lady also a guy? Will the salutation of future business letters be "Dear Guys"?

One of the early morning TV network show hosts wished, "Happy Mother's Day to all you guys!" Does anyone even think of what she's saying?

At my first yoga class, the instructor greeted the class by saying, "You guys are gonna catch on fast." I looked around. Not a guy in the group. Whatever happened to "you ladies"?

Back when I lived in the Midwest, I thought I was becoming comfortable with being *one of the guys* until my church group held its last meeting of the year. It was the treasurer's turn at the podium. "I want you guys to know how much your donations have helped," she bellowed to the assembly of over three hundred women.

Recently, at a tony restaurant specializing in Mediterranean cuisine, my husband looked distinguished in his new jacket, button-down shirt and tie, and I wore an elegant black dress. "Hi, you guys, what can I get you?" the waiter asked, oblivious of our appearance and age.

Later, we found out he was a foreign exchange student. First thing they must learn when they come to this country is to address everyone as guys.

In my opinion, "you guys" subtly reduces everyone to a common denominator. The appellation ignores individuality as well as status earned through hard work and dedication. You are just a guy; you deserve no special respect or consideration.

Should I care? Do you?

Well, you guys, what do you think?

# 34

# NOSTALGIA

*From: Peggy*
*To: Cassie, Barb*

*Dear friends,*

*I'm writing to you at 2:40 in the morning because I woke up from nightmares and cannot get back to sleep. This is happening more and more. A few hours of sleep and then I wake around 2:00 or 3:00, and I'm up the rest of the night. Usually, I just lie in bed, my mind racing from topic to topic.*

*It's chronic angst that wakes me. Once disturbed, I think about all the undone things on my interminable list (no, I'm still not cured of this, even though I know better), about my son and granddaughter, about my mother's mental health, about my aging body, about the disruptive high school kids who come into the library more to socialize than to study—Cass, you must face the same thing where you teach—about* how precarious life is and how we're all just sitting ducks for the evildoers of this world.

Tonight, however, I decided to get up and turn on the all-night oldies radio station, low volume so the music won't wake Mack. Bittersweet memories are flooding my mind as I type, and I'm thinking of missed opportunities and past mistakes

Physicists say that once things have been in contact, they always in some sense remain connected. A change in one thing, or person, can create a simultaneous change in the other even if they are separated to the opposite ends of the universe. I see Trent's face. Nostalgia rules.

From: Barb
To: Peggy
Cc: Cassie

Peggy,

I just checked my e-mail and read your message this morning.

I wish I could have come over and turned off your radio last night. You're in heat! Go get yourself some hiking boots and walk it off!

Sometimes we can be aggravated with our true loves for a period of time—weeks, even months. You've heard the one about the woman who had been married for thirty-one years to a great husband who suddenly seemed like a stranger to her. "Right now, we're redecorating," she explained to her friends. "When we're through with this project, I'm sure I'll be able to say once again that he's a great husband, but not now."

*It isn't Mack you want to get away from so much as it is the stresses currently at work in your life. The intense feeling of longing is not to be confused with actual love itself.*

*Don't misinterpret your sense of longing to mean that you must have Trent. There is always a sense of longing in all of us.*

*To paraphrase C. S. Lewis, that's because we were created for another home. These are but the shadowlands, the real life comes later.*

*End of sermon.*

*Ciao, caro e meraviglioso signore.*


<u>From: Cassie</u>
<u>To: Peggy</u>
<u>Cc: Barb</u>

*I just got home from school and I'm wiped out. As is my habit, I checked my e-mail right away.*

*Listen, you're wandering about in times that don't belong to you anymore. Get back to the present.*

*From: Peggy*
*To: Cassie, Barb*

Tonight while I was prepping dinner and carefully removing my store-bought tomatoes from their vines, I had a sudden flashback to a parallel moment when I was about nine years old. I was sulking about some triviality when my dad motioned for me to join him in the vegetable garden in our backyard. As we picked the ripest tomatoes from their vines and placed them in the waiting basket, he said, "Smell the tomatoes; now, don't you feel better?"

So . . . I smelled the tomatoes. And then I thought of all the blessings in my life.

Our sense of smell does have curative powers.

Love you both.


*From: Barb*
*To: Peggy*
*Cc: Cassie*

First, let me say that I'm glad you are feeling better now than you did last night.

Remember back in the spring when we talked about all the annoying changes in our lives and you mentioned the comeback of some of your old menopausal symptoms like mood swings and raw nerves at times?

Your body is still adjusting to being without hormone therapy. I think this is at least part of the reason you have *been feeling so restless this year. A free-floating, generalized anxiety is an unpleasant burden and can make a woman much more vulnerable than she normally would be.*

*We all look back on our lives now and then and wonder what would have happened if we had taken a different path. Yet that different path would have led to other issues and multiple unknowns.*

*Taking off my nurse's cap, I want to just say, as your friend, that temptation can exert an irresistible pull. Close that door and don't walk through.*

*Ciao.*

# 35

<u>Peggy'sMoments.com</u>

## CATCHING FIREFLIES

### Third Saturday in December

The comeback of so many of the songs from decades ago, used in current movies, plays, and commercials, makes me nostalgic about the summers I spent while growing up in Indiana. Those summers of firefly-catching contests or talking the evenings away while sitting on the front porch were not supposed to end.

Funny how certain moments from the past stay with us as vividly as if they just happened. I can still remember a profoundly strong feeling that suddenly came over me one night when I was about twelve or thirteen. It was the middle of a hot sticky summer, and the only thing on my schedule that night was catching more fireflies in my jar with the punch-holed lid than my friends could get. I had perfected the art of focusing on one specific lightning bug at a time as it glittered. Then, at the precise second it lit up again, I'd snatch it with my right hand.

Since my jar was the first to be totally filled with fireflies, I won the game. Then, as always, all of us opened our glass baby-food jars and watched as the tiny beacons flew away, flashing their lights. (We valued those little insects, without knowing that one day some scientists would extract the substance that produces their light and use it to try to track and destroy cancer in human cells.)

On that one particular night, as I watched the last firefly break free from my container, a sensation washed over me—that time and possibilities were everlasting. Although I was realistic enough to know that my wonderful summer would, in fact, end, I felt as if a layer of peace suddenly had been laid on top of earthly time limitations. I savored the feeling until I fell asleep hours later that evening.

Now, I find it difficult to focus on one thing at a time. Typically, while I'm trying to accomplish a task, dozens of thoughts about other subjects dart in and out of my mind. Even when I'm working out at the health club, I can't fully enjoy the experience. I'm thinking of what I've got to do next and checking my watch at sporadic intervals.

*Flashes of light. That's what our lives are. Look, they're here; look again, they're gone. Just like the knack for catching fireflies, you've got to concentrate hard, then grab for the moments of light that the people in your life emit.*

As carefree and unencumbered as my youthful summers were, they also were sweltering and humid in the years before relief came from air-conditioners or those large window fans our dads proudly installed. I'd lie awake at night for hours, clad in sleeveless, shortie pajamas, flat on my back, barely able to breathe, skin glistening with perspiration.

And sure enough, just as I would finally start to feel sleep taking over, the perpetual mosquito would locate me. The high-pitched *zzzzzzs* as the insect circled above my exhausted body would jolt me awake just as the bloodsucker started its kamikaze dive. Pulling the sheet over my head with just a small air hole, I'd wait for it to give up and leave me alone.

Do I really want to go back in time to my childhood home?

I recall a lady who called the popular radio show, *Car Talk*, one day. She told the hosts, lovingly known as *Click and Clack,* that she had felt nostalgic right before "an important middle-aged birthday" and had decided to purchase a Volvo just like the one she had driven in 1961. She bought it on the internet for three thousand dollars.

"The ad said it was in perfect driving condition, but the brakes don't work," she wailed.

Click and Clack's answer: This just goes to show you can never go back home. And in this case, she can't even get out of the driveway!

# HOMESICKNESS

If you ask me what I'm most wistful about, I have to say my kind, loving, gentle father. During my growing-up years, the world would stop for one magical span of time every evening, shortly after my dad's arrival home from the business day. Led by him, the dinner table would then become a forum for dissecting and analyzing the day's happenings, social issues, news events, and ethical dilemmas.

If a neighbor *just happened to drop by* during our dinnertime, which frequently occurred, he would warmly tell them, "Pull up a chair, have something to eat, and see what you can add to our discussion."

Adult visitors would eye with anticipation the jug of wine my dad always kept underneath the table, take a position on the topic of the day, and plunge unabashedly into full debate. By agreeing to disagree, young and old alike found these dinner discussions informative, provocative, and entertaining.

He instilled in my sister and me that life is a gift from God to be lived to the very best of our given abilities with love for others and with appreciation. To this day, whenever I'm feeling down and out, I can hear his advice, "Make sure you find at least one person each day you can help or lift up. Do this, and you will soon feel well again."

Back in time, I can hear us singing together as he played his mandolin or laughing so hard we couldn't stop during a game of cards. And I can hear him describing the gamut of colors in a landscape, the intricate webbing of a leaf, the perfect geometric design of a dahlia, or the majesty of a tree.

In my mind's eye, I can clearly see the two of us walking along the beach during summer vacations and talking animatedly about anything and everything, just as my friends and I do now. Oh, how I miss our conversations!

Another thing I miss about my childhood is our unlocked doors. From the time we got up in the morning until bedtime, my parents kept both the front and back doors unlocked. It was not unusual for us to arrive back home after an outing and discover a friend or neighbor patiently waiting in the living room for our return.

"Well, finally, where have you been?" one of my mother's friends would always ask, as if my mother knew this particular woman might make an unannounced appearance at any time and, therefore, should always be present and available. This expectation was not so unusual since my mother treated each one of her countless friends as if she were her very best friend. They would come for her counsel, her wisdom, and her uplifting attitude.

I like to picture my mother, ready to attend some gala event, dressed in a gown of imported fabric and impeccable workmanship, resplendent in a wide range of colors that flow one into another. Her hat, shoes, and handbag are the perfect finishing touches. And when I look at her beautiful face, she is smiling her marvelous smile.

I also recall the anticipation of going to the drugstore on Saturdays to buy the latest *Little Lulu* comic book and a chocolate ice cream soda. With my fifty cents allowance, I felt on top of the world.

Which of your treasured memories make you feel nostalgic?

# 36

# CHRISTMAS WISHES

*From: Peggy*
*To: Cassie, Barb*

*My dearest friends,*

*I know we've already exchanged gifts and cards, but I wanted to touch bases quickly before Mack and I pack our suitcases for our annual pre-Christmas visit to my mother and Mack's side of the family in Indiana. Of course, we'll be back in time to celebrate Christmas Day here with our son, daughter-in-law, and granddaughter.*

*Thank you again for continuing to buttress me during an emotionally challenging time. You both are busy getting ready for lots of company, but if you get a moment, take a look at my blog about catching butterflies. Christmas seems to go hand in hand with nostalgia, and my story is meant to stir beautiful, cherished memories in those who read it.*

*This is also a time for one-to-one kindness. It is much harder to give of ourselves to one flawed relative or acquaintance than it is to dispense money to a cause or charity, where we never have to look anyone in the eyes, smell their sweat, or worry about whether they have similar values. Christmas helps us polish our manners and our patience.*

*May peace and joy reign in your hearts. Merry Christmas and Happy New Year! See you in three weeks.*

*Love and Friendship,*

*Peggy*

# WINTER

*Walk and be happy; walk and be healthy.
The best way to lengthen out our days is to walk steadily
and with a purpose.*
—Charles Dickens

# 37

# HE KNOWS!

*From: Peggy*
*To: Cassie, Barb*

*Dear Cassie and Barb,*

*He knows! Somehow Mack knows!*

*This afternoon, after a frustrating day of trying to write and hitting a blank wall, I thought I'd just take a quick look at my inbox before driving to the beach to fast-walk a few miles and try to relax. As I scrolled down the list of junk mail and forwarded a couple of good jokes, there before me was an e-mail from Mack sent at 12:30, during his lunch break at the financial seminar he's attending this week.*

*That's right! From my very own husband! It was short, so I copied it below for your eyes only.*

From: Mack
To: Peggy

Dearest Peggy,

I love you with my whole heart and mind and soul and strength.

Mack

---

*Why would Mack send me this e-mail, and why at this particular time? This is the first time Mack has ever in his entire lifetime sent me an e-mail.*

*Quite a while ago, before we bought our new computer, Mack used to occasionally check my e-mail as a favor when I would get backlogged. But ever since I reduced my library schedule to three times a week instead of five, I've had sufficient time to keep up with my own correspondence. Anyway, we've got different e-mail addresses and passwords; I don't think he even knows mine, and he's not a snooper.*

*Of course, Mack knew that I went to my college reunion three months ago. Mack was playing in a tennis tournament here that same weekend and happily packed me off to meet with my old sorority sisters. That's it! There really has been nothing to arouse suspicion.*

*Maybe I've been acting differently?*

*From: Barb*
*To: Peggy*
*Cc: Cassie*

Dear Peggy,

Smells can give you away.

Odor communicates between people. We take in odor messages with our breath, decipher them, and react accordingly. We smell differently when we're happy and centered than when we're anxious or under stress. Mack probably smelled your anxiety.

Even sickness has its own smell. As a nurse, I know this firsthand. I can smell when Drew's coming down with something, and I tell him so every time. "You can't smell my bug if you've got a cold yourself," he always chirps back, his eyes dancing with mirth.

Smells aside, Mack is perceptive. Just as you would sense something amiss with him, so he sensed it with you; you know each other so well.


From: Cassie
To: Peggy
cc: Barb

Never mind how he knows.

With an e-mail like that, anyone could fall in love all over again!

# 38

# MOVING

*Always do what you are afraid to do.*
—Ralph Waldo Emerson

"We've really got to downsize to a one-level house, it's time, and I'm dreading all the work and inevitable hassles involved in the whole process of moving," Barb vented.

"Moving's a beast!" Peggy concurred.

Barb elaborated. "Of course, the first challenge is *where do we go?* Surely not into the neighborhood Drew and I looked at the other day, where every single backyard has a swing set except for the one behind the house that is up for sale."

"Maybe that's why it is for sale; the owners need some peace and quiet," Cassie laughed, as they headed away from the Strand, a concrete strip that doubles as a main street along the shore in Oceanside, and down to the palm-lined beach. It was a chilly January morning, and the three friends had layered their clothing accordingly.

From one end to the other, the sky resembled an immense canvas that some gigantic artist had primed with a dull grayish color in preparation for painting a winter scene. The mist blurred the horizon line so that the ocean appeared to melt into the sky.

"All the newer housing developments I've looked at so far are predominantly occupied by young couples with screaming babies and skateboarding adolescents. Been there!" Barb resumed.

"Why can't I find a newer North County coastal development where the demographics are more evenly spread out—some young families, yes, absolutely, but also some empty-nesters, and some active retirees like Drew and me?"

Barb's pitch shot up a couple of decibels, revealing her frustration. "I keep reading about the ever-increasing numbers of people whose ages fall somewhere between the end of middle age and the beginning of elderly. Where, oh where, do they all live?"

"Maybe they're in Bhutan, the last of the Shangri Las," Peggy chuckled, as they walked briskly past a dozen or so sanderlings scurrying along the shore's rippled waterline.

Cassie, who had been intently listening to Barb and Peggy up until now, finally asked the obvious question, "Would you consider one of the adults-only communities?"

"I'm not ready to be boxed off from the mainstream cross-section of humanity," Barb practically barked. That was that.

"It's true that the newer housing developments are a magnet for growing families," Peggy agreed. "Which means you might want to check out some of the older housing developments where the kids have already grown up and their parents have remained."

"Or," Cassie quickly added, "you might find a house you like in one of the more established, free-standing neighborhoods that are not part of a planned housing development. There are plenty of good neighborhoods like this with a nice generational mix."

"So it's going to boil down to a tossup," Barb sighed, kicking a broken clam shell out of her way. "For me, living in a newer housing development has a definite edge over residing in an older neighborhood. This means I'll just have to settle for probably being the oldest homeowner on my street. I won't like that a bit."

"Why not?" Peggy shouted over the sound of a crashing wave. "You could go outside to water all of your potted plants with frizzy hair and no makeup on and on one would even care. They'd be wrapped up in their own competitive spheres. You would gain a priceless feeling of privacy and freedom.

"Add to that the extra layer of safety in a neighborhood with a high level of visible, audible activity.

"Anyway, Barb, you're already immersed in the overall community, so you'll continue to have access to people within a wide range of ages and stages no matter who lives or does not live on your street. It really won't matter," she encouraged.

"How do you feel about leaving your current neighborhood?" Cassie injected.

"Like an awkward, vulnerable child who's about to venture into unknown territory with all its complexities." Barb suddenly slowed her pace, and the others dropped back enough to stay aligned with her.

"Okay, but you do realize that part of the fun of life is you never know what's around the next corner," Cassie smiled. "Change makes us know we're alive.

"Back when I was married, I lived in the same neighborhood for over twenty years and you know what? Neighbors came and went, trees were destroyed by storms, and a new shopping plaza was plopped right at the entrance to our housing development. The neighborhood did not stay the same just because David and I stayed there all those years. And we certainly didn't stay the same," she added with a smirk.

"On a humorous note," Cassie continued, "I remember having to fill out my home builder's survey when moving into my townhouse six years ago. My real estate agent kindly sent her assistant over to help me unpack. Anyway, when I got up to the question, *Why have you relocated here?* she suddenly blurted out the answer, '*Federal Witness Protection Program!*'"

After several loud bursts of laughter that startled a Speckled Godwit as the bird pecked at its irresistible morsel, Peggy resumed the subject of change. "As I've said before, it's an illusion that change is suddenly thrust upon us, and we are victims having to adjust. Actually, each moment is unique and never happens again.

The only difference with your upcoming change is that it will be more dramatically obvious.

"When Mack was climbing his business ladder, we were beckoned to several different cities, finally ending up here nineteen years ago. As much as I always abhorred the work involved in moving, once we settled in, I fully enjoyed the subtle and unique differences in each location."

By now, Barb was starting to relax and feel better. Her tense shoulders dropped at least an inch, and her arms swung freely once again as the three women strutted with a quickening pace toward the pier, where they would enjoy a refreshing drink before going home.

At that moment, Peggy thought of the one greatest relief and profound satisfaction that she personally would derive from the whole process of moving (if she had to move), and practically sang it out to Barb.

"Just think of all Drew's stuff you'll be able to finally get rid of!

"You'll be packing so many boxes he won't know one from another. You can easily slip two or three boxes of his stuff out of your house each day and drop them off at the dump. He'll never miss any of it. Lucky you!"

Peggy watched as a wide grin crossed Barb's face and thought to herself, *This almost makes me wish I were the one moving!*

# 39

# PEGGY'S PINK LADIES

On Tuesday afternoon, just as Peggy finished adding a library patron's name to the long waiting list for a new book, she looked up from her desk behind the long counter in time to spot a young woman approaching with flowers.

"I have a delivery for a Ms. Crawford," she announced, placing the floral arrangement near one end of the counter.

"Really? Well, you've got the right person."

"Enjoy."

As Peggy got up to pull out the card, she was struck by the number of exquisite Pink Ladies, which dominated the spectacular display. These had been her favorite of all the proteas from the time she had vacationed in Maui with her parents and sister during the summer of her junior year in college. *Who would possibly remember this*, she asked herself, knowing the answer. And as she silently read the words, her heart leapt.

> The buck is on one side of the stream,
> The doe is on the other.
> He looks at her full of yearning,
> Their eyes meet.

> She stands so close and yet so far.
> Will she cross the stream?
>
> Trent

She could leave the flowers in the library for book lovers to ogle, or . . . Quickly, while no one needed assistance, she sent a text to Cassie.

> A magnificent floral arrangement was just delivered to me at the library from you know who. It breaks my heart to look at them. Can you swing by and pick them up? I would feel better knowing my good friend, who loves flowers, is appreciating their beauty. I remember how much you admired the intricate designs of the dahlias and other prize-winners at the Del Mar County Fair last summer. Just so you know, we close at five today. Thanks so much.

Forty minutes later, a text from Cassie signaled its arrival with a few musical notes.

> Will be on my way right after my last class. Try to enjoy your proteas until then.

# 40

_Peggy'sMoments.com_

## TAKE IT ALL IN

### January

*In all things of nature there is something of the marvelous.*
—Aristotle

During my cooldown along the beach, just before sunset one evening, I tried to take it all in—the majestic beauty, the marvel, and the mystery.

> The setting sun played hide-and-seek with cloudlets,
> Spattering their fringes with embers of yellow-orange and red.

As I walked at a slower, more reflective pace, I fantasized that the uncountable grains of sand that supported me represented parallel universes, zillions of parallel universes.

I thought about *Horton Hears a Who* and worlds within worlds. Maybe we're in a universe that is within something else much larger that we cannot even imagine. Relative to infinite space, our universe could be like Horton's dust speck which would make us smaller than quarks, a millionth of a billionth of a billionth of a billionth of a centimeter. And yet, we have this strong sense of our own importance.

> The setting sun crept along the beach and o'er the sea.
> In the dusk half-light, around sand and water,
> Seagulls pierced the sky like phantom shadows.

From these thoughts, my concentration shifted to the scene about twenty yards ahead. As I slowly approached, I could see that some two dozen seagulls had formed a circle around a gloriously all-white, massive seagull. The towering bird was eating a big chunk of fish that had washed up on the shore.

Close by its side was another seagull that acted like a bodyguard, flapping its wings and lunging at any of the other gulls who tried to take a quick bite of the morsel. Finally, when only a little bit of fish was left, the loyal bodyguard seagull attempted to take his well-deserved reward. But the kingly seagull let out a piercing screech and actually pecked his own body guard. Though he was satiated, he would not allow his loyal comrade even one small taste of the good life.

*Amazing*, I thought, *they are like some humans . . . but not all, not all.*

I circumvented the seagulls and continued to walk, pondering why we humans are compelled to gaze at the water so much. I knew exactly what Barb's husband would answer, as quickly as a flash, "Well, we're 80 percent water . . . and the majority rules!"

> The setting sun slowly, silently, slipped under the horizon line.
> The glory of the moment swelled my heart
> Like rediscovered friendship long forgotten.

Scattered kelp bulbs popped underneath my weight as I approached the parking lot. A homeless man, wrapped in a worn blanket, pulled a bit of soft bread from inside the roll he was eating and offered it to a hungry sandpiper. *No, not all are selfish,* I rejoiced.

> The evening breeze, a barely audible laughter,
> The gentle lullaby eternal of the sea,
> Kept whispering, "Take it in,
> Take it all in,
> Take it all in!"

# 41

# SPEAK, WRITE, THINK

"It seems as if every day I'm hunting for some misplaced item, either in the house, garage, car, or my purse," Barb mused. "Of course, Drew doesn't mind at all; he hopes I'll also misplace his to-do list of projects."

"Fuzzy memory," Peggy said. "We used to hear about it from our parents and grandparents Funny how what happens to everybody else can, and actually does, end up happening to us too."

Their offhand remarks gave Cassie the perfect opening to jump right in. "The one best way to remain mentally sharp throughout our lifetimes is to make the effort to speak and write with accuracy and precision. Speaking, writing, and thinking are so intertwined that if we get sloppy in one of these abilities, the others are affected.

"While I was teaching English grammar to a freshman class last Thursday, one boy raised his hand and complained in front of the whole class, 'But nobody talks that way so why are you bothering to teach us this?'

"Unfortunately, he was partially right—almost none of the kids and fewer and fewer adults speak well anymore. At one time, good grammar was stressed all through elementary and high school.

Those who went on to college started with a firm foundation in the English language.

"These days, though, I'm trying against all odds to teach correct grammar, sentence structure, and a richer vocabulary. Many teachers don't even bother to correct grammar, spelling, or punctuation errors in their students' papers. They turn a deaf ear to spoken and written sentences that start with 'Me and her . . .' Appalling! How will today's kids be able to write convincing business letters when they start working?"

"So how did you respond to that boy's question," Peggy asked.

"'Just think,' I told my class, 'if people were able to put their deepest emotions and feelings into words, there would be less misunderstanding and much more harmony in the world. Also, by making the effort to find the best words and construct sensible sentences for our mixed-up feelings, we would gain a better understanding of ourselves.'"

The three friends were sitting at an umbrella table outside of one of the many Starbucks shops that dot coastal North San Diego County. They had already taken a long walk and, since it was still early in the afternoon, had decided to extend their time together.

Cassie continued. "Online games—in which pixilated flesh and blood characters can be created in a virtual reality—are okay up to a point but can usurp far too much time. Where's the balance between time spent with iPads, iPods, and iThingies and time spent reading well-written books and learning to express one's thoughts with some creativity? How do we coax today's kids out of their electronic cocoons long enough for that?

"Nicholas's grandson, the one who just got his learner's permit," she related, "was getting in some driving practice with him recently and was stunned at his calm reaction when another driver almost backed into them in a parking lot. 'Don't you ever curse or use bad words, Granddad?' he asked.

"Nicholas answered him with a rhetorical question: 'Which reaction would that careless driver remember more: *Where did you get your license . . . at Walmart's?* or a stream of F-words and B-words?'

"The English language is going down the drain just as many traditions are. Yet, ironically, being able to communicate effectively is our best fortification as we age and our physical strength starts to wane.

"Even for practical, everyday life, persons of all ages need to expand their vocabulary. Just saying 'It hurts' is not enough information to enable a doctor to help you. Is the pain steady, shooting, stabbing, sharp, or aching? Or are you feeling soreness?"

"It's not just the general population who are losing the art of precise speech," Peggy weighed in, almost knocking down her coffee with a quick wave of her right hand. "Is there anyone left in the media who speaks English correctly?

"Here's what drives me crazy. One TV news anchor starts using a particular catchword or phrase and then everyone else in the news business jumps on board.

"Someone stumbles upon a word, others hear it and become enamored of it, and then we have to hear that word fifty-five times a day. Count how many times the word *clearly* is used in just one typical news report or feature story. *At the end of the day* is a phrase currently in vogue. These words and phrases are fine to use occasionally, I use them myself, but when they are used too often, they become distracting."

"Broadcast journalists and public figures repetedly make mistakes with basic grammar—forget advanced grammar—just very basic grammar, which is easy to grasp and to use," Cassie added. "Instead, they should go out of their way to speak correctly. After all, they provide the example that most people naturally follow."

"Cassie, nobody's keeping track of the state of English grammar today, except maybe a few teachers like you and a handful of professional writers," Barb insisted.

Peggy resumed, "The politicians should do better too. A world-renowned congresswoman often says *crisises*, instead of *crises,* the correct plural of *crisis.*

"Mistakes in everyday, ordinary conversations are expected. It's the blatant mistakes on the written page and the mistakes in a public speech that are hard to swallow."

By this time, Cassie was speaking louder and faster but didn't care. People already had left the tables nearest them. "The authors and editors of many current best-selling novels either don't know or don't care about correct usage.

"Certain grammatical mistakes have become ensconced in everyday speech to the extent that the mistakes now sound right and the correct words sound wrong. I feel like I'm losing the battle to keep our language from disintegrating further," she sighed.

"Okay, you two," Barb grinned, "since we're on this subject, let me tell you my English language pet peeves. Worst of all, in my opinion, is the substitution of the word *discomfort* for the word *pain* by the medical profession? As I let out a scream during my recent sigmoidoscopy, the attending nurse inquired passively, 'Are we having a bit of *discomfort*?'

"And how can a meal be *healthy*? The meal itself does not have good health; it is good *for* your health. A meal is *healthful.*

"Also, have you noticed that nobody *disappears* anymore? Now, they *go missing.*"

It was time for a little levity and Barb continued to provide it. "I've got to guiltily admit, though, that *thing* is my most useful, nondescriptive word. The other day, I simply said, 'Oh, this will make a great *thing* to clean the *things* with.' The great *thing* was a torn tank top that I used to exercise with and the *things* were the toilet, the shower door, the tile in the bathroom, and the mirrors.

"Of course, Drew didn't know what I was talking about. He simply nodded and said, 'I'm glad your *thing* is still working for you.'"

"Most amazing to me," resumed Cassie, not skipping a beat, "is the resurrection of the word *cool*. That was our description of everything from boyfriends to chemise dresses to sub sandwiches when we were teenagers. The runner-up for best descriptive word is *awesome*. No wonder when I try to expand their vocabulary by teaching adjectives, the kids in my classes stare ahead blankly."

Barb asked, eyes still twinkling, "What about the overused word *hot*? Who determines whether something or someone is cool or hot? That is the big question."

Cassie finished her coffee and ordered a second one. "Look, we all want to evade fuzzy thinking as we celebrate birthdays. You want my recipe for a good mental exercise to keep our brains young?

*"Think.* A technology author, by the name of Nicholas Carr, worries about what the internet is doing to our ability to concentrate, what with all the hypertext links, new mail pings, and blinking banner ads. We are flitting like hummingbirds from apps to tweets to search engines to YouTube.

"*Write.* Go ahead and write all those letters to your loved ones you've always fantasized you would write. Write to your representatives and senators and leaders whom you admire and encourage them with your words.

"*Speak.* This is the time in our lives to speak out. What about all the things your conscience is yelling at you about? It used to whisper and gently nudge; now, it's screaming. You know exactly what needs speaking up about.

"My dearest friends, your words are the links to spheres of inner knowing.

"Remember: No matter what you say or don't say, write or don't write, there will be criticism from some. So you might as well do what's right, and deep down in your heart and soul you know what that is, and then leave the results to your Creator.

"*Speak well. Write well. Think well.*"

# 42

# REALIZATION

<u>From: Peggy</u>
<u>To: Cassie, Barb</u>

*My Dearest friends,*

*You will be relieved to know the wheel-spinning and chasing of my own tail stops right now.*

*Since I would never be content with a* same-time-next-year *arrangement with Trent, I have either got to be with him completely or be with Mack 100 percent. Either—or—but not with both of them.*

*With Trent, there would be the excitement of starting over, building a new life, everything fresh and new. There would be mutual admiration, passion, and constant mental stimulation.*

*Mack is Dr. Seuss's Fix-It-Up Chappie, come to life. He easily could have been an electrical or mechanical engineer, even a plumber, instead of an accountant. Mack is not brooding and mysterious, and he doesn't quote Shakespeare or Milton. He's definitely not a romantic. When we were young and in love, he did not pop the question on bended knee; he simply left some brides' magazines in my car with a note on top asking, "Which one of these gowns is you?"*

*On the other hand, Mack has always been there for me, my rock through storms and challenges, as well as the joys of life. And he will always, without a doubt, be there for me in the future, no matter what. Mack says what he means and means what he says. He is guided by principle, not preference or whim.*

*I realize that the initial excitement with Trent would wane, and then we would start the inevitable process of doing the work involved in building the kind of relationship that Mack and I already have.*

*There would also be so many incidents that would automatically trigger memories of Mack and me. That would be torturous.*

*Besides, Mack loves me with his whole heart and mind and soul and strength.*

*I think you know my decision.*


From: Cassie
To: Peggy
Cc: Barb

*Enjoy your marvelous all-around man, Peggy.*

*For anything that needs fixing around here, I either have to figure it out myself or call a handyman service. According to Nicholas, all you need to run a household are duct tape, WD-40, and white distilled vinegar, and that's what he brought over last weekend when I mentioned I was going to have to get something fixed.*

*Nicholas is entirely lost when it comes to technology. "I can't get out!" he kept frantically repeating from downstairs the other day, till I finally ran down to see what on earth was happening. What he could not get out of was the menu for programming a show on the VCR. He couldn't find* Quit *on the new remote and was quite worked up—this normally calm, cool, and collected man.*

*I am delighted for you and Mack.*


<u>From: Barb</u>
<u>To: Peggy</u>
<u>Cc: Cassie</u>

Something tells me that Mack's e-mail note to you was the beginning of many new and surprising discoveries about Mack that you are about to embark upon.

Buono decisione! I couldn't be happier about your decision.

Lots of love to you and Mack.

# 43

# TRENT'S DREAM

*From: Peggy*
*To: Cassie, Barb*

*I am sending you both a copy of Trent's response to my decision. It makes me feel gut-wrenchingly nostalgic.*

Dear Peg,

I respect your decision, but if you ever change your mind, I'm here for you. Mack is one lucky man.

> Sometimes I dream we're on a journey
> Whose destination is nowhere,
> Where time perception vanishes.
>
> Sometimes I dream we fly beyond
> The misty borders of the universe,

Beyond the twilight zone, the stratosphere.

For always and ever,

Trent

*From: Cassie*
*To: Peggy*
*Cc: Barb*

Just sing a few rounds of the oldie, "Na, na, na, na, hey, hey, hey, goodbye," and it will become impossible for you to feel sad. You'll see.

*From: Barb*
*To: Peggy*
*Cc: Cassie*

Trent's first poem to you about the buck and the doe now has an ending.

> The doe gazes across the stream no longer,
> But turns around resolutely.
> Eyes dancing with mirth,
> Her pace quickens toward her destiny.

Ciao. See you soon.

# 44

# GREEN-EYED MONSTERS

*I think everybody should get rich and famous
and do everything they ever dreamed of . . .
so they can see that it's not the answer.*
—Jim Carrey

"The best thing happened at school this week." Cassie could hardly contain her enthusiasm as *the walk and talkers* waited impatiently on the beach for a noisy helicopter to whiz by.

Smiling victoriously, she continued, "I was actually able to stop *jealousy* dead in its tracks.

"Ever since second quarter started, I've noticed an escalating pattern of the same three girls in one of my English classes targeting a certain student for their jealous venom. At every possible opening, they make disparaging remarks or cast nasty looks her way."

Cassie elaborated as they kept walking in unison, arms swinging naturally at their sides. They had reached a part of Solana Beach covered with pebbles, polished stones, tiny crab and lobster shells, bamboo shoots, and driftwood discharged by impetuous waters during the winter months. It was the first Saturday in February.

The tide was at its lowest so that there was plenty of room between the water's edge and the high cliffs.

"By last Monday, I realized things were getting worse. I spotted my good student at lunch break, sitting alone at a table, making no eye contact, and hurrying through what must be the most agonizing period of her school day. Every once in a while, the clique looked over at the solitary figure and let out a mocking cackle or rolled their eyes.

"You should know that the girl they've singled out is attractive, smart, and has a special talent for creative writing. Apparently, these three little green-eyed monsters resent her success and also must sense a gentleness of spirit that won't fight back," explained Cassie.

"Little by little, they were turning their chosen victim into the school pariah—someone whom no one else would dare befriend. Such is the force and momentum of envy. Well, I made the decision that this was not going to continue, not on my watch!"

"What did you do?" Barb and Peggy asked, almost together.

"I played my hand on Wednesday as I calmly wrote on the board, *Today's Writing Topic*: *If you came to school one day and suddenly your friends wanted nothing to do with you, poked fun at you, looked down on you, what would you feel like? Provide descriptive details. If this continued, how would it change you? How would you start acting? Would you ever be able to stop it? How?*"

Cassie paused to catch her breath, then trumpeted, "Bottom line, no one has bothered her since!"

"Your writing topic forced the class to put themselves in someone else's position. Great, Cassie," Peggy said.

"I endured a similar experience as the girl in your class, only I didn't have a teacher like you." Barb suddenly said in a serious tone, looking in Cassie's direction.

"I never knew you went through anything like that," Cassie replied.

"Ancient history," remarked Barb, "but I must admit it took a few years for the clique's negative remarks to stop replaying in my mind."

"Did you ever get over your hurt feelings and justifiable anger?"

"At some point, I made the decision to go ahead and forgive everybody everything. As soon as I did that, I freed myself to attend reunions and thoroughly enjoy hearing my former classmates' life stories and future plans. Only one or two of the ones who were particularly nasty ever showed up, and after a civil hello, we just didn't bother with one another."

"My grandmother used to tell us that some of the women in her region of Italy wore strands of garlic around their necks to protect them from the ill will of others," Peggy informed. "They called these necklaces their *contra malocchia*. Of course, they worked, probably because no one would want to get near the overpowering odor of the garlic.

"Looking on the other side of things, jealousy is not exactly beneficial for the persons who are feeling it either. It's like an acid that eats away at their well-being, rots their spirits, and imprisons them in bitterness. They are filled with a nagging sense of yearning that can never be satisfied, no matter how many of their dreams come true.

"It can actually become a lifestyle, can even dominate the personality to the point where there is always something to be jealous of—wealth, fame, talent, personality, looks, whatever."

"Right," agreed Barb with a mischevious tone, "and jealous of those with cast iron stomachs that can digest anything, those who have perfect in-laws, those who globe-trot every few months, and those who never wash their hands and never get sick. Then there are the women with husbands who cook, clean, plus fix everything in sight, and the superwomen who only need five hours' sleep at night to run circles around you."

Peggy joined in the fun. "Add to your list someone who writes the great American novel while commuting to work in a carpool, someone who speaks five languages fluently, and someone who can stay calm and cool as their diamond ring drops down the sink drain, their washing machine stops working during the first of eight loads, and their thirty-nine-year-old son calls to say he has just filed for bankruptcy—all on the same day."

"Whenever I start to feel a twinge of envy toward someone," added Barb, "Drew's sage advice comes to mind: 'You can't just pick and choose something about someone else and allow yourself to become envious of them. You've got to take their entire package, every single other aspect of their life. Would you really swap?'"

"I know what we wouldn't get jealous of—someone who has more debt than we do," Cassie laughed.

"If someone seems to have it all, I just figure, *Let them enjoy the short, precious time that all is going well in their life*," mused Barb.

"One way to stop feeling jealous is to reverse it," suggested Peggy. "Instead of cutting someone down with hurtful remarks, say something nice. Build up the object of your envy.

"There are times of suffering and pain in everyone's life, only the details vary. So why not be delighted for your friends and relatives when things are going well, why not enjoy their good times with them.

"My mother always said, 'Be jealous of no one, ever. Compete with yourself. Like yourself. Be yourself.'

"Really, though, the best antidote for envy I've ever heard is *want what you have*. That simple yet profound philosophy was the legacy handed down by my great-great-grandfather.

"Coffee aficionados are content. They look at their coffee, smell it, take a sip, and say, 'Ahhhh!' Look at your home, garden, clothes closet, stocked refrigerator, yourself, your loved ones and say, 'Ahhhh!'"

Cassie slowed to a stop, picked up a shell, and studied it. "Look at the intricate design of this cockleshell with its radially ribbed valves," she said, holding it up for Peggy and Barb to examine.

"I've asked the kids in one of my classes to bring in two or three shells next week. Their assignment is to describe each of their shells in exact detail, paying attention to color, size, shape, texture, pattern, type, and any unusual aspects. This exercise should sharpen their descriptive writing skills," she explained.

"Great idea for one of your vocab lessons," said Barb.

"Here's a shell with seaweed attached to it," observed Peggy, scooping it up. "I'd say its structure is layered and its shape is coiled."

"That's the idea," Cassie said with satisfaction. "One of my favorite shells is the Jingle. You see them only once in a while. They're tissue-paper thin and either gold or silver."

"Almost makes me want to start a seashell collection," smiled Barb.

Peggy was driving north along the Coast Highway when her thoughts drifted back to her Conch shell experience about a year ago.

On that particular day, she was feeling despondent and decided to take a long walk by herself along the beach to assuage her emotions. As she walked, she came upon a sight she would always remember.

Conch shells, washed up on the beach after a storm the night before, were strewn about everywhere. It was highly unusual to see so many shells of the exact type in one location, all within about fifty yards of each other and the thought crossed her mind that this phenomenon could be a sign meant to encourage her.

Peggy carefully picked up the marvelous swirled shells, a few at a time, and placed them in a safe spot adjacent to the rocks. There were nineteen in all. Then she jogged to her car, procured a canvas bag from the trunk, and hurried back to collect the treasure.

She still had them at home in a large, clear glass vase, and they comprised one collection she would never give away or dump.

# 45

<u>Peggy'sMoments.com</u>

## LEGACIES

### February

More than a century ago, my great-great-grandfather Pietro built an abode from straw and clay on a sliver of land in Abruzzo, Italy, for his seven children, his wife, and himself. His humble *pinchara* had one room for sleeping and the other for cooking, cheese making, bread making, meat smoking, and chestnut roasting. At night, the family huddled around the hearth to soak up its warmth and talked and sang to distract themselves from the cold.

What possible legacy could this very poor man have left that still survives for so many generations? In what way does he continue to inspire his descendants?

Pietro's essence is captured in one of my father's poems, entitled "Nonno Pietro," which appears in part below.

One day, the son who had improved his lot
Asked Nonno to move to his shining new house:
"There are rooms to spare, it's modern in style."

Nonno Pietro flashing a broad smile,
"But why would I?" he said to his son.
"How can life get better than this?

All the comforts I need are here,
Here, in this glorious pinchara:
My daily loaf of crusty bread,
My daily bottle of fine red wine:
The vision of my family 'round the hearth,
My bride, my children seven—all of them—
Memories of strife and pains,
Losses and gains,
Strength, love, and joys.

You see, my dear son,
How can I leave all of this?
How can life get better than this?"

What a beautiful legacy Pietro left! *Want what you have! Be thankful for the gift of life. Choose to dwell on all that is good and wholesome and beautiful. As to the rest, accept and adjust.*

Pietro remained in excellent health, working on his farm and driving horse and buggy to the market, until one fateful day when he tripped on a stone while walking, fell, and broke his hip. He never fully recovered (the best medical care was not available) and just slipped away at ninety-four.

## FAVORITE STORY ABOUT PIETRO

Pietro had a special method for disciplining his four sons. Whenever one of them misbehaved, he would wait until the middle of the night. Then, he would get up, quietly pull up a chair alongside the boy's bed, tap him on the shoulder, and begin to talk.

He would talk on and on, in a low, calm voice, until they would say, "I give up, okay, you're right" and beg him to just let them sleep. If they started to doze off, Pietro would tap, tap, tap them on the shoulder again and launch into part two of his lecture.

He would let them know exactly what they had done wrong, why it was wrong, and how they could improve. No arguments ever occurred because his sons were too tired to formulate one, and Pietro never once raised a hand against any of his sons.

Pietro wanted a captive audience who could do nothing but listen. During the day, when growing boys are so easily distracted, it would have been a waste of his time and energy to try to keep their full attention and extract a genuine promise to improve, and he had much work to accomplish before the sun set.

How wise of Pietro!

## 46

# HOUSEWORK . . . UH, OH!

*The invariable mark of wisdom is to see the spectacular in the common.*
—Emerson

"Guests are coming from out of town next weekend, and I don't feel like cleaning the house; I'd much rather indulge in some chocolate cake and go shopping for a pair of stylish platform heels," Barb stated in a flat tone of voice shortly after they started to walk.

Cassie and Peggy laughed and nodded their heads.

"Once you pass *go*, you'll get the job done," Cassie encouraged. "Just get into a slouchy outfit, gather all of your cleaning supplies, strut into your master bathroom, and close the door behind you. Cleanup guaranteed . . . works every time."

"Drew's solution for my lack of enthusiasm about tackling the bathrooms is even better*: Rent a Johnny on the Spot and place it outside on the patio*, snickered Barb.

The rhythmic ebb and flow of the ocean combined with sand patterns that resembled a quilted bedspread put Peggy in a relaxed, comfortable mood. She could not believe it was already the third Saturday in February.

"Of course, you both realize that doing housework is déclassé," Peggy teased. The confused expressions on her friends' faces begged a full explanation.

"Don't you realize it's socially incorrect to admit to cleaning your own home? You know who's still in the closet today? Homemakers, that's who.

"According to the current repressive social code that governs housekeeping, it's okay to have an interest in fashionable furnishings or creative cooking, both of which imply status. You may also brag or complain about your cleaning service or your maid if you employ one. And it's become admirable, even trendy for a man to scrub, vacuum, and dust.

"There was a time, before the 1970s, that women openly discussed *spring cleaning* and exchanged tips about the efficacy of baking soda and white distilled vinegar for cleaning. Now, though, if such unintellectual drudgery as housework is undertaken, it is apparently accomplished in secret because no one ever breathes a word about it."

"Well, *anything* can be considered either as drudgery or as interesting," Cassie inserted. "Attitude rules! Cooking can be resented and hated or considered a creative activity, a hobby even. Laundry can be therapeutic, a time to think. Straightening the closets seems to parallel a cleaning out of the cobwebs of your mind."

"The great thing about doing the laundry," Peggy hastened to add, "is the immediate satisfaction of a job well done. You see, smell, and feel the results—hear the humming of the dryer, swishing of the washer.

"The first, last, and only time I got a maid, I not only straightened before she arrived, so she could get started immediately, but I went around the house after she left with a toothbrush for all the corners she missed," Barb said.

"Besides," she added, wrinkling her nose, "I really don't want to chance anyone coughing or sneezing all around my house. Even if a maid looks healthy enough, she might be a 'carrier' of who knows what. And do they ever wash their hands?"

"My mother had the same maid for many years," Peggy related, "but she worked side by side with her to be sure each job was done the right way and that there was no 'wheel-spinning.' I remember Mom saying there are two types of cleanliness—surface cleanliness and hygienic cleanliness. In other words, don't take the same rag you wiped some slop off the floor with and then use it to wipe off the kitchen counter. Everything can look clean and neat, but it can actually be harboring a disproportionate number of microbes.

"When the time comes that I need maid service, I'll get it. Right now, though, I can handle the routine cleaning I'm left with after having the windows, carpets, and floors professionally done once a year. So far, so good."

"My wish upon a star is a perfect house, every minute of every single day," Barb said wistfully. "Drew says this can happen. No problem. All he has to do is buy the house next door. That would become our model house, perpetually ready for guests and entertaining, while our current house would remain as is, for normal everyday living."

"Since I can only afford one house," Cassie smirked, "the answer for me is just to keep housework in perspective. I mean, the sun won't crash into planet earth if I don't clean the chandelier. But when I do decide to clean it, I'll turn up my favorite music, throw myself into the job, and, *gasp,* enjoy it.

"And remember, we are not dragonflies—the only creatures able to move in any direction with breakneck speed and force. Multitasking for humans can be overrated at times."

Waving goodbye to her friends, Peggy thought, *Let's be grateful we can take care of our homes. Someone in a wheelchair would give anything to be able-bodied enough to do the household jobs women complain about. This is what I'm going to think about the next time I vacuum behind and under the furniture.*

# 47

# A FULL PROPOSAL

*"We cannot live for ourselves alone. Our lives are connected by a thousand invisible threads, and along these sympathetic fibers, our actions run as causes and return to us as results."*
—Herman Melville

<u>From: Cassie</u>
<u>To: Peggy, Barb</u>

*Dearest friends,*

*As you know, Nicholas has never tried to bring up the subject of marriage again, ever since I brushed him off last December. We have just continued to see each other at least a couple of times a week as if that awkward scene never even happened.*

*So you can imagine my quandary when he suddenly stopped calling or seeing me without any explanation at all for one long, lonely week. Try as I might, I couldn't figure out why.*

*Then he showed up Thursday night, without phoning first, calendar in hand as he walked into my living room.*

*"Which of these dates would be best?" he asked.*

*"What on earth are you talking about? Best for what?" I asked in return, arching my eyebrows.*

*"Of course, the date actually depends on how much preparation time you need for everything to be exactly the way you want it to be." His answer was a non-answer.*

*I looked at the calendar. It was one of those monthly calendars, where you have to flip over the pages to move from one month to the next. It was already opened to a date in May. A circle had been drawn around the eleventh with a bright red pen.*

*"One possibility," Nicholas said.*

*Then he turned the page to June. The first week of the official start of summer was highlighted in yellow. As I kept staring at the date with a slow but sure dawning of its significance, Nicholas said, "Would the anniversary of the first time we met work for you?"*

*Well, dearest friends, I've given you a blow by blow account of Nicholas' revised proposal. As for my answer? I'll let you know when I see you tomorrow at the beach.*

# 48

# HAPPY MARRIAGES

*Laughter is the closest distance between two people.*
—Victor Borge

"So what was your answer?" Peggy and Barb shouted as Cassie sashayed toward them with a Cheshire cat smile. It was early March with spring scheduled to begin in just a few days.

"How would you both like to meet me at my favorite dress boutique next weekend?" Cassie replied, with an impish facial expression.

Picking up on her friend's mood, Peggy teased back, "Why ever would we want to do that?"

Cassie threw back her head and giggled. "Why to pick out the dresses you'll be wearing at my wedding, of course."

In no more than five seconds, Peggy and Barb hugged Cassie and then the three of them formed a circle, arm in arm, rejoicing and laughing.

"And guess where we're going for our honeymoon?"

"Where?"

"Texas. I'm going to get a western hat and boots and do some serious line dancing down there."

When they finally started their walk, Cassie filled in the details. "The advice you gave me amounted to more than just vanishing puffs of air," she explained. "I absorbed it and had a lot of time to think during the week that Nicholas didn't call me. I realized that I love him so deeply I would take care of him anyway if he ever needed special care, whether I stayed single or not.

"When I said yes, I swear I could almost hear that old song, ' . . . sooner or later, love's gonna get you,' playing in the background.

"I also realized that a sense of humor is one of the secrets of a happy marriage, and that's something both Nicholas and I have. He enjoys referring to our initial meeting as *love at first impact*. If my ex and I had been able to pull back sometimes and just laugh at ourselves, probably we'd have lasted. After all, we are but actors in our own daily sitcoms, and we're the stars of the show.

"Another beneficial ingredient in a solid relationship, whether you're married, dating, or engaged like me, is having at least one interest or hobby in common, even though you're interdependent," she continued. "Both Nicholas and I thoroughly enjoy live symphony performances. The last time we went to one, we were about twenty minutes early.

"'They're just practicing, practicing, practicing,' I said impatiently, referring to the cacophony of musical sounds. 'Isn't it a little late for that?' Nicholas chuckled."

"What else makes for a good marriage?" ventured Barb. "Let's explore this a bit."

"Separate bathrooms!" was Peggy's automatic reply.

"Definitely," concurred Barb, "that and a zillion other things.

"Drew's wit greatly enhances my ability to enjoy life. Recently, when I fussed about his not listening to half of what I say, he merrily responded that he listens to the other half.

"And then just the other day, I complained, 'It's as hot as a mausoleum in here! You should have opened some windows if you shut the AC.'

"'It's a preview of coming attractions,' quipped Drew."

After cracking up with laughter, Cassie regained her composure enough to add, "Drew could provide copy for the top stand-up comedians."

"Another thing, we don't have long arguments. Whenever we're angry with each other, I start rearranging the furniture, and Drew takes a walk. Over the years, he's developed quite an appreciation for nature.

"This is not to say I don't get annoyed with Drew. Since he retired from the PR firm last year and started consulting from home, he's got something to say about every single thing I do or don't do. I'm planting irises and peonies, and he wants a different color arrangement; I'm cooking and he stands over me, *Gourmet Magazine* in hand, telling me to add this or that. He wants us to do more entertaining. Sure, I'm the one doing all the work. Then I have to listen to his critique after our guests leave.

"When I get irritated with Drew, I like to repeat Joyce Meyer's line to myself: *You might as well keep the one you've got because you're going to have to work on the next one too!*

"Mack gets up from bed about every two hours for what we've dubbed his *night walks*," Peggy said, "for obvious reasons. I only need to get up once, now that I've stopped drinking liquids after seven. Anyway—it was bound to happen—we finally collided one night, and both of us broke out into the longest, hardest, loudest laughter we'd shared in weeks."

"If I start fuming about what Nicholas has or hasn't done," inserted Cassie, "he keeps quiet and lets me own the floor until, at some point, I realize I'm simply arguing with myself. He figures that anything he says will be wrong, that I will seize upon a word, a phrase, something, and then the argument will begin in full force.

"I have to admit he's right. Once, while I was still pouting after a disagreement, he said, 'You're beautiful.' My angry response, which, unfortunately, we both still recall, was 'What do you mean? I don't even have on any makeup!'"

"Cell phones," Barb blurted out. "Cell phones can promote happy marriages.

"If Drew is not in the exact same room as I, even if I can see him from where I am standing, and I try to tell him something I think is important or at least interesting, I always need to repeat it or walk over to where he is. His excuse is that I'm not in his hearing range (although he claims to have perfect hearing). So now, if I'm in the kitchen and he's in the study, I just press speed dial.

"When he's immersed in reading and I tell him how much I love him, he responds with a 'Ditto' or an 'I love you too.' Anyway, I finally told him I need to hear a lot more than that at this stage of my life. 'Sure, honey, double ditto,' he murmured."

"That's just Drew being Drew," Peggy said

"I don't think I ever told either of you," Barb went on, "but when I first met Drew, I was already engaged—long distance—to a young man in Ireland. In one of his romantic and poetic letters, he wrote that we were meant to be much more than *ships passing in the night.* That letter captured my heart.

"When I bragged about the romantic letter, Drew snickered and said, 'His ship passed. Mine stopped!'"

"Glad you brought up romance," Peggy chuckled. "The best prelude to a romantic evening for me is the sound of the shredder."

"You mean the shredder turns you on?" laughed Cassie.

"Listen, whenever Mack actually gets rid of some of his stuff, especially his disorganized paperwork, he can skip the candlelight, music, and everything else."

Peggy's remarks got Cassie thinking. "There's an art to appreciating the quirks and imperfections in one another and in shifting our focus from what is wrong to what is right. The Japanese call it *Wabi Sabi.*

"I think what the three of us have with our men are similar values and morals. We relate with them spirit to spirit, soul to soul. I've always said love is not enough. A husband and wife also need to like and admire each other."

Peggy quickly agreed. "What Mack and I have started to do every night during dinner is give thanks for at least five things that happened during our day. This simple habit is helping to keep us more connected.

"*With a Song in my Heart* was playing on the radio the other day and I thought how apropos it was for happy marriages. May our hearts keep singing for the ones we love!"

As soon as Peggy returned home, she started to prepare *Spezzatino of Veal,* a recipe her father had passed down to her and one of Mack's favorite meals.

She placed a pound of veal, already cut into small pieces by the butcher, and half a pound of assorted mushrooms into a large pan and sautéed them in olive oil and butter until the veal turned golden in color.

Next, she added an eight-ounce glass of dry white wine, garlic, rosemary, salt, a little black pepper, and a dash of Worcestershire sauce. Covering the pan tightly, she cooked all of the ingredients over a very slow flame.

Soon, the irresistible aroma reached out, pulled Mack away from his paperwork, and propelled him into the kitchen. As he sliced the crusty Italian bread waiting on the counter, Peggy continued to frequently stir the veal until almost all the liquid evaporated.

Mack dressed the crispy salad of fresh endive, radicchio, and escarole and carried it to the dining room table as Peggy filled their plates with the piping hot veal specialty.

This was the beginning of a glorious evening together.

And much later on, the bedroom door closed.

# 49

# LOVE AFTER FIFTY

*A woman who could always love would never grow old.*
—Jean Paul Richter

<u>From: Peggy</u>
<u>To: Cassie, Barb</u>

*Dear Cassie and Barb,*

*My new Adirondack chairs and garden settee were delivered today, and I had the pleasure of tucking them cozily among the tumble of bougainvilleas and pots full of colorful flowers in our backyard.*

*I enjoyed helping some hardworking, respectful sixteen-year-olds who were working together on a project this week at the library where I work, and Mack took the initiative of buying tickets to see a Neil Simon play next weekend.*

*Barb, you were right about surprises yet to come!*

*Thank you, thank you, thank you, my friends, for helping me stay on the right path during a tumultuous time in my life.*

# 50

# THE BEST IS YET TO COME

## Third Saturday in March

*The friends thou hast and their adoption tried,
grapple them to thy soul with hooks of steel.*
—Shakespeare

Peggy watched as a long white line of surf stretched like an artery down the beach at La Jolla Shores. As a dozen or so pelicans flew in formation above her, she thought of the uplifting power and energy that Cassie, Barb, and she provided for one another through their enduring friendship.

As each pelican flaps its wings, it creates an uplift for the bird behind it, she noted. Traveling on the forward movement of each other, they get to their destination quicker and easier. Each pelican takes a turn in the lead position with the ones behind honking their encouragement.

And when a migratory bird gets sick and falls out of formation, two birds follow it down to help and protect it. *They're just like us; we stand by each other like that. The joy of life within each of us is contagious, and when we occasionally are gripped by some unhealthy emotions, we act as filters for one another.*

As the pelicans disappeared from view, Peggy turned to see Cassie in one of her tea-length beach dresses approaching with a bouncy kind of walk, her long chestnut-brown hair blowing in the gentle breeze.

All smiles, she announced, "Nicholas and I have decided on a small wedding, followed by a reception at his house since that's where we will be living. His floor plan wraps around a central courtyard with an outdoor kitchen, fireplace, and fire pit, so it's perfect for entertaining."

"Great," Peggy said, "and have you chosen your wedding dress yet?"

"Yes, and you and Barb and Nicholas will all see it for the first time at the wedding."

"Ah, secrets."

Barb leisurely strolled toward them. "So what are we talking about today?"

"Before you two arrived, I was thinking about our friendship," Peggy said.

"What I love about our friendship," said Barb, "is that we openly communicate without restraint about every topic imaginable, letting our feelings and beliefs flow. We look and really see, we listen and really hear, and we appreciate each and every moment from the ordinary and routine to the over-the-top ones. You, my dear friends, rejuvenate and animate me."

"Did you know," Cassie asked, "that grapes are like sponges? They sensitively absorb tinges and hints of earthy information that resides in the soil where they grow. They are able to convey wonderful tastes to sensitive palates—of fruits, spices, shells, woods, and microorganisms that have been in the soil around them for millions of years.

"Like grapes, we have soaked up lifetimes of information and wisdom to share with each other."

"So what you're saying is that we are grapes? What else are we?" Peggy chirped, as the three of them locked arms and continued to chat and laugh their way along the water's edge. Puffy clouds formed a white canopy over the indigo ocean, and the stunning natural beauty made the three of them feel as if they were on a mini vacation.

"We've come so far this past year, haven't we?" Peggy pondered. "We've grown into better and stronger women with so much to celebrate. I for one came back to my senses and realized I would have just been shifting things around if I had started a new life with Trent.

"No matter how perfect he seemed while I was enthralled with him, he eventually would have exhibited little habits, characteristics, or inclinations I wouldn't have liked. Veneers always lose their luster. So I would have exchanged Mack's traits for another man's mannerisms.

"Love is a decision, and thanks to you both, I made the right one."

"I want to say the very same thing," Cassie said. "You two helped me get over my fears and embrace the miracle of totally unexpected love."

"The love we give will be our very best legacy," commented Peggy.

"Remember how overwhelmed I used to be about all the age-related changes in my life?" Barb asked. "Now that I've learned how to balance the demands of others with the new and exciting things I want to do, I know I can handle whatever the future dishes out. You should see my desk right now with all the brochures and books about Italy spread out. In only three more months, my granddaughters and I will be on our way.

"And . . . I'm happy to let you know, Drew and I just made an offer on the perfect smaller house for us.

"Life will continue to have twists and turns, surprises, delights, challenges, and changes. We'll be making adjustments the rest of our lives."

"Right," agreed Peggy, "and we're up for it."

"Oh, I have something else to tell you," said Cassie. "I have also decided to stop teaching at the high school and to do private tutoring instead for persons of all ages who take the initiative to learn, who really *want* to learn. No more force feeding! A tutor, that's who I really am."

*Do we ever get to the end of ourselves, become fully ourselves?* Peggy couldn't help but wonder. *We're always in the act of becoming, from conception onward. With spring around the corner, I am curious about what else is around the next bend. What I do know is that we have many more miles to walk and talk.*

As they approached their parked cars, Peggy suddenly had an idea.

"Wait a second," she said, while unlocking her Toyota and reaching inside for three water bottles.

"A toast," she smiled, handing one to each of her friends. "To all of our surprises and adventures ahead!"

"Absolutely," said Cassie, twisting off the cap.

As the three bottles clicked together, Barb trilled, "And may we laugh exuberantly, laugh long, and laugh often."

Anyone within earshot of Peggy, Cassie, and Barb could hear their cheerful voices singing that wonderful song of Mama Cass's: "Make your own kind of music, sing your own special song . . . sing it strong, to last your whole life long."

# 51

_Peggy'sMoments.com_

## UPLIFTING SONGS

Here are some of the most encouraging and inspirational songs ever written, along with a sprinkling of a few upbeat songs that are just plain fun to sing along with.

I Believe

You'll Never Walk Alone,

Somebody Bigger Than You and I

Make Your Own Kind of Music

The Impossible Dream

You've Gotta Have Heart

Through the Years

Climb Every Mountain

It's My Turn

I Am Woman

I Remember You

What a Wonderful World

Stand by Me

Turn Around Look at Me

If You're Going Through Hell

You can find the songs and lyrics online.

Enjoy!

# AUTHOR'S NOTES

My three main characters are a composite of many good friends with whom I have enjoyed countless stream-of-consciousness conversations over the years about the endless topics that comprise our everyday lives. Their cumulative wisdom and ability to make adjustments to whatever life dishes out are etched in my memory.

Our current walk and talks continue to refresh, embolden, and inspire me with new ideas.

Many thanks to my marvelous husband, whose positive attitude and ever-ready quips provided the copy for Drew's hilarious one-liners. Some of the poetry is from my late father's beautiful collection of poems. I also appreciate the kind friends and loving family members who have cheered me on.

A very special thank-you goes to the multitalented songwriter and singer Anna Wilson for her outstanding theme song for this book.

As baby boomers approach sixty, and with ten thousand persons every day turning sixty-five and women living longer lives, there is a huge and increasing market for realistic fiction that validates fifty-plus women and does so in an entertaining and fun way. They are the new protagonists capable of carrying the weight of a story line by themselves.

CPSIA information can be obtained at www.ICGtesting.com
Printed in the USA
BVOW071151171212

308282BV00002B/39/P